W9-CCP-777

DANGER BOY

DANGER BOY

Dragon Sword

Mark London Williams

CANDLEWICK PRESS
CAMBRIDGE, MASSACHUSETTS

This is a work of fiction. Names, characters, places, and incidents are either products of the author's imagination or, if real, are used fictitiously.

First Candlewick Press edition 2004

Library of Congress Cataloging-in-Publication Data

Williams, Mark London.
Danger Boy : Dragon sword / Mark London Williams. — 1st Candlewick Press ed.
p. cm.
Originally published as: Dino sword. Berkeley, Calif. : Tricycle Press, 2001.
Summary: Twelve-year-old time traveler Eli Sands continues his search for his missing mom, encountering new characters and trying to save the free world from tyrannical rule.
ISBN 0-7636-2153-6
[1. Time travel — Fiction. 2. Science fiction.] I. Title.
PZ7.W66697Dan 2004
[Fic] — dc22 2003055338

10 9 8 7 6 5 4 3 2 1

Printed in the United States of America

This book was typeset in Slimbach Book.

Candlewick Press
2067 Massachusetts Avenue
Cambridge, Massachusetts 02140

visit us at www.candlewick.com

For Dick and Deb,
my first Bay Area
tour guides, with love

Prologue

The Lake

The old king stands by the lake, looking over it as for the last time, waiting.

Waiting for a woman. A woman who's never touched land.

After a moment, she appears from under the water, calmly floating up, then hovering just over the surface. The woman remains utterly serene, as if rising from a lake then standing above it were scarcely remarkable. She seems very patient, as though she could wait a long time to take tired kings into her liquid embrace, take them into the lake with her when their hearts are broken for the last time.

This king is very tired. He's seen too much war, too much bloodshed—and knows he's caused a lot of it.

When he was younger, he never thought he'd wind up hurting like this. He thought everything would be perfect.

The king is going to throw the sword into the lake, let this water sprite have it, because this sword, it seems to him now, is the root cause of all his misery.

He remembers pulling it from the rock when he was younger; he remembers thinking it would make him invincible.

That was a lie. It only made him king.

Now, no more lies. Just water. And silence.

He holds the sword above his head, ready to fling it into what he thinks will be its final resting place.

"Arthur."

It's Merlin's voice. The old wizard is always

speaking at moments like this, breaking the king's concentration, never quite taking anything seriously enough.

This time Merlin's pointing. Out at the water. The serenity is even draining from the Lady of the Lake's face. There's a swirl of foam and bubbles next to her, and something unexpected. An intruder.

It was just supposed to be the king and Merlin here, alone with the water sprite, to dispose of the sword. The sword and a whole lot of bad memories.

But there's someone else. Someone who's kind of . . . fading in. *Thrashing about in the water, gasping for air, trying to swim.*

Is it another wizard, here to challenge Merlin? Or perhaps a spirit, the wandering ghost of some man killed by the king in a forgotten war?

The king can't tell. But Merlin doesn't seem worried. He seems, in fact, slightly amused.

But then, Merlin always seems amused, no matter how bad the situation.

The small caps and breakers in the lake are

shredded apart by the frantic splashing as the intruder buzzes through the water like a small, agitated shark.

As the trespasser draws near, the king lowers his sword and lets it rest in the mud by his leggings.

It's a boy coming to them. Out of the water. A boy.

Soon to be a man, but not quite.

About twelve years old.

Wearing jeans and a baseball cap—though the king wouldn't have the faintest idea what to call them.

"Hello," the boy finally gasps.

"Well met," the king says. "Or, perhaps, not so well. Merlin, is this one of yours?"

The boy looks from one man to the other, then back at the king. "Arthur?" The boy speaks with the strangest accent the king has ever heard.

But the conversation is interrupted. The water starts bubbling and churning again. And another boy begins fading into view.

Chapter One

Eli: One Man's Family

December 24, 1941 C.E.

"Mom?"

I'm standing in front of a big hotel up on a hill in San Francisco. The Fairmont. The sign matches the name on the tattered piece of paper in my hand. I've just walked across the city. It's cold and it's night and it's Christmas and the United States has just plunged into a world war.

And my mother stands there shivering, with tears running down her face.

"Mom?"

I don't know what else to say right now. I'm kind of stuck at "Mom," which itself is a word, a name, I haven't said out loud for a long time. Because there hasn't been anyone I could say it to.

Well, I guess it's not really a name. It's more a title. Her name is Margarite. Margarite Sands. She's my mother, and she disappeared in an explosion in the year 2018. An explosion that threw her backward in time.

Of course, I've come backward in time, too. To find her and bring her back. Back to my dad. To her own world.

"Eli? Is it you?" At first she reaches out like she's going to touch my face. Then her hand just stops there, in midair, frozen. Like maybe I'm a ghost, or a mirage. A Christmas ghost.

But a ghost from her past or future?

Even I can't quite figure it out.

It takes another moment for her fingers to reach my face. She brushes my cheek, then takes her hand away, satisfied that I'm still standing here.

"It's me, Mom."

She's quiet again, all bundled up in her coat—a coat I've never seen before.

She's older than last time I saw her, too. She has a scarf around her face, so it's hard to tell what the difference is—maybe the expression in her eyes.

She's been away from me longer than I have from her. On my long walk over here, I saw the holiday decorations, and a couple of people wished me "Merry Christmas." I finally checked a newspaper. It's December 24, 1941.

My mom has been back here since at least 1937. So practically five years have passed for her. She's five years older, and I'm not.

Getting tangled up in time—traveling from one time to another—does funny things like that.

"How did you find me?"

"I was about to go inside when I saw you getting off that cable car."

"No, I mean how did you *find* me? Back here. In"—she has to think about it for a split second—"1941?"

I hold up the paper. It's Fairmont stationery, with the word *help* written on it in her handwriting. It appeared inside the time sphere in my dad's lab.

My dad, Sandusky Sands, is a physicist. So's my mom. One of their experiments about slowing down time got out of control, and a lab blast hurled her back . . . to here. To right before World War II. Except it's not "before" anymore. Europe's already at war, and now the U.S. and Japan are, too.

After Mom vanished, Dad and I left our home in Princeton, New Jersey, and moved out West. He'd inherited an old winery, close to San Francisco, in the Valley of the Moon. About fifty miles north. And a million miles away. Dad is still living in 2019.

He tried to stop all his research then, shut the whole thing down, but he was basically forced to continue by DARPA, the Defense Advanced Research Projects Agency, and one of the guys who runs it, Mr. Howe.

Howe made sure that all the equipment Dad

would need to keep doing his experiments was sent west, too. Dad realized the work on time spheres was going to go on with him or without him. And without him, it would be a lot less safe—for whomever else Howe got to do the work, and for the rest of the world.

Of course, Dad had already lost Mom. And then I got unstuck in time myself. And he doesn't want to lose me, too. But he hasn't. He won't. I'm coming back.

"I can move around in time, too, Mom. I can even control it now. A little bit." My hand touches the small metal disk in my pocket. It's a chrono-compass Dad's been working on. Between that and my supercharged baseball cap, I'm a regular one-man time-ship. I can cross the Fifth Dimension to go to different points in history. Though it takes a toll on your body. For me, I'm always left a little woozy.

"Oh, Eli." Mom's sounding a lot more sad than happy. "It can't really be controlled. And you shouldn't be here now."

"You mean on Christmas Eve?"

"I mean during World War Two. For America, it started two weeks ago. Officially. Right after Japan bombed Pearl Harbor. Hey"—she leans over and touches my forehead, though this time it's like she knows I won't disappear—"you're sweating."

"Yeah, I'm—" I want to tell her it's the effects of the time travel, but she's already worrying like a mom. "I had to walk a long way to get here."

"But it's forty degrees out. You should be shivering, not sweating." Well, she's sounding like a mom, too. Then she finally gives me an all-out hug and kiss. "I can't believe you're here."

"Are you glad?" She hasn't said she's happy to see me yet.

"I don't know." The hug winds down, and she's looking at me again, getting all concerned.

She doesn't know? Aren't mothers always supposed to be glad to see their children, no matter what? No matter how dangerous things are?

Or are parents willing to be sad, to be in pain, if it means their kids are safe somewhere? Is that what it means to *be* a parent?

"Is your father here?"

I'm about to tell her, *See? It'll be all right, he's waiting for us,* that the whole idea of my coming back was to bring her home with me—when the air is filled with the loud wailing of what sounds like a million ships blasting their horns out at sea. Or maybe thousands of those old-fashioned gas-powered cars, like you see in history vids, all honking at once.

But these aren't just horns. It's a more . . . *panicked* kind of sound.

"Air-raid siren," Mom says. "Come on."

She takes me by the hand and pulls me into the hotel. In the lobby, people are scurrying around, some of them holding their ears, but no one is diving under tables or anything.

"Are we about to get bombed?" I yell over the noise.

She shakes her head and pulls me through the crowd. Farther across the lobby, there's a large Christmas tree with tinsel wrapped around it but no lights. A big poster is propped up in front of it with a picture of Santa Claus arm in arm with Uncle Sam:

PUT COAL IN DER FUEHRER'S STOCKING!
BUY WAR BONDS!

I wonder who "der Fuehrer" is. Mom motions for me to keep following her across the lobby. We pass a ballroom and I glance in, then stop: There seems to be some kind of play happening onstage. Or at least there had been, until the sirens brought everything to a halt. There's a small orchestra, and the whole room's decked out with holiday decorations. Leading the band is a little man with fuzzy white hair—except they're not playing right now, and his baton seems frozen in the air. Onstage, actors in tuxedos and evening gowns are all gathered around . . . what? Metal poles of some sort, with small cages on top.

There's a woman near the entrance dressed like a large elf, or Santa's helper. She's passing out small gifts from a big red bag. She doesn't seem fazed by the air-raid sirens at all. She smiles and thrusts one of the objects into my hand. It's a small mirror. Around the frame, there's writing: "You are reflected in your friends, family, and times!" it exclaims. "*One Man's Family* on NBC Radio."

Radio! That was like the audio part of a vid-screen, without any pictures. I bet those poles are for voice recording and they're doing a show in there. I think.

I want to ask Mom, but she points to her ears—it's still too loud to talk—and motions toward a door. It opens to a staircase.

It's cold in the stairwell. After a few flights, I huff out another question. I'm full of them. But you would be, too, if you hadn't seen your own mom in five years. Or even two. "Doesn't the elevator work here?"

"Too crowded," she says. "We're going up

to my room." We're speaking to each other the way my friend Andy and I used to, when we'd keep the background music to a Barnstormers game turned up: Our conversations would be normal, except that we were nearly shouting at each other, in a casual way.

"What about the sirens?" No one else seems terribly worried, but I've read about World War II. It was a horrible time almost everywhere, and I don't remember if San Francisco was ever bombed or not.

"It's just a drill. They announced it on the radio."

Like fire drills at school. You know ahead of time they're coming. I always wondered if that destroyed the whole point of practicing—you're not really responding like you're supposed to, like you would if it were the real thing.

We stop climbing when we get to the fifth floor, then walk down a carpeted hallway to room 532. She stops. There's a wrapped present with her name on it in front of the door. She looks at it, shakes her head, and quickly picks it up, then takes out a key. It really is a key, not a card, and she uses it to open the door.

As suddenly as they began, the sirens stop.

"Home for the holidays," Mom says, motioning for me to go in.

I step inside. Her room is small but not too messy—there's a bed in one corner, a desk, and a little kitchen area. But I don't know how she cooks anything. There's no oven, and no microwave fiberwrap to heat up food.

There's no Comnet screen anywhere, either; no rain alarms to warn about sudden storms, no bug sirens for stray bacteria and viruses—it's like the old West.

It is the old West.

"Wow, Mom. So what do you do up here? Do you have one of those televisions?"

"No." She smiles and shakes her head. "I listen to the radio. I read and draw."

I show her the mirror. "Radio? You mean audio, right? Is that what they were doing downstairs? But don't you have a Comnet—"

"It's that thing over there." She points to a large, curved wooden cabinet with a kind of grill in front of it.

She turns it on. Nothing happens.

"It takes a minute to warm up." She takes off her coat, scarf, and mittens. I'm just wearing an overshirt and jeans. Mom was right: I'm cold, in spite of the Fifth Dimension sweats.

"Did you say you draw?" She never drew before. I guess she really is here all alone.

"I've had time to learn some new things." And then she looks at me. Long and hard. Even more intensely than the way she looked at me down on the street. It's a look that I probably wouldn't understand if I were still a little kid.

It's not just an "I'm your mom and I've missed you" look but something more. Not even one of those "God, how you've changed" looks that you get from other relatives. It's both of those, and something else. I don't know if

I can describe it. I said it was intense, but there's also that . . . *regret* is the word that adults would use. Like you want to take back something that you did, but you can't. Like she might not get another chance to stare at me that way again.

Except she will. Because I came here to bring her back to her home-time. Where she belongs.

"Because it's never an interruption when it comes to America's safety!"

I jump. A man has just started speaking in the back of the room.

"That," Mom says, "is the radio."

"So hurrah for the sirens and drills! And now, as the Fairmont's own Samuel Gravlox Orchestra plays our show's 'Destiny Waltz' theme, we return you to the elegant, windswept Sea Cliff area of San Francisco, for more heart-rending, day-to-day adventures of the Barbour clan in this holiday broadcast of . . . *One Man's Family*!"

"That's what they were doing downstairs," she tells me. "They're broadcasting live from the hotel. *One Man's Family.* It's a huge hit. They're doing shows from all over the city this week. They're tying it in to selling war bonds."

"Wow. . . . So those big metal things were the microphones? For digitizing their voices?"

"Well, they don't digitize, but yes, those were microphones."

"So what are war bonds? And who's 'der Fuehrer'?"

"Oh, Eli, honey." That's not what she wants to talk about. "Who sent you here? I know your father wouldn't do it."

"No one sent me. . . . It was my idea, and I came myself. I can move through time on my own." I point to the Seals cap on my head. "With this."

"With a baseball cap?"

"Dad says it all has to do with particles. With those WOMPERs. Those Wide Orbiting Mass Particle—"

"Mass*less*. Wide Orbital Massless Particle Reverser. That's okay. I could never have remembered the whole thing either when I was . . ." Her eyes widen a little. "How old are you now? How long have I been gone, for you?"

"I'm twelve now, Mom." Now it's my turn to feel sad.

"Twelve. Well I guess I owe you a couple of happy birthdays."

I don't know what to tell her. I don't know if I'm supposed to say that it's all right, that it's not her fault. Or maybe she needs to tell me something. Neither of us speaks right away.

"No, Eli. I couldn't have said it at twelve, either. Of course, WOMPERs weren't even discovered until I was in college." She says it like she's trying to tease me. The way she used to. I guess we'll talk about the missed birthdays later.

"Dad says I'm like one big WOMPER charge myself—when the cap comes in direct contact with me. It's shielded now, but when it touches me, we fuse together to become like a giant positron—"

"Shooting backward in time," Mom says. She doesn't seem overjoyed by any of this. "How did that happen?"

"Another accident." Which I helped cause by reaching for the cap when it popped into Dad's time sphere in the first place. But I don't think I'll mention that just yet.

"And where is your father now?"

"Back home. Waiting for us."

She sighs and sits down in a big antique chair. Though I guess here it's not an antique yet. "How is he?"

"He misses you."

She doesn't reply. "Come look," she says. She takes some sheets of paper out of a drawer and lays them on the table. "These are my drawings."

I gasp. They're me. *Me.*

Except *older.* Like in high school or something. Sitting in a chair. Waving. And playing baseball in Herronton Woods, back near Princeton.

"Since I couldn't see you growing up, I

tried to imagine it," she tells me. "I would try to picture it in my head, then draw it. So I could keep connected to you somehow. So I wouldn't lose you completely. That's how I learned to draw. That's why."

"You're not going to lose me, Mom. I'm here."

"I'm glad you haven't grown quite as much as I thought."

"We don't live in New Jersey anymore, though. We moved."

There's so much she doesn't know about me and Dad now.

"You moved?"

"To California."

"Where? Here? San Francisco?"

"Close by."

"Well, sit down and tell me all about it. We'll spend Christmas Eve together. That will make me happy." She gives me another smile, and this one seems full out, with nothing else behind it. "We can make warm Ovaltine!"

"The chocolate stuff?"

"It's real big back here. Kids like it. The company makes decoder badges and other things for prizes. The boys pretend they're Captain Midnight. That's the big radio show Ovaltine sponsors."

"Captain Midnight and Danger Boy," I say, trying it out. Sometimes it feels like I've fallen into a comic book, except that people I love and care about are in real danger.

"Who's Danger Boy?" Mom asks.

"I'm still trying to figure it out," I tell her. I don't mention it's a code name that Mr. Howe thought up for my DARPA files. Then, thinking about comics and chocolate sparks another question: "You get a lot of kid visitors?"

"I'm a teacher, too, Eli. There's a school in the hotel for the families who live here." She takes out a glass jar of milk from her tiny wooden-looking refrigerator. I wonder how they made electric appliances out of wood.

"Mom, we don't have to spend Christmas Eve by ourselves. We can go back right now. To 2019, where you belong. It's still fall. You can get ready for Christmas all over again, with Dad and me."

The smile that was sneaking back on her face when she was talking about the hot chocolate is gone now. "Eli, it isn't that simple."

"Why not? As long as you're holding on to me when I put on the cap—"

She shakes her head.

What possible reason could she have for not wanting to come home?

I don't even want to know. Except I have to.

Before I get the chance to ask, there's a frantic knocking at the door.

Chapter Two

Eli: Samuel Gravlox

December 24, 1941 C.E.

It's the man with the bushy white hair from downstairs, the one leading the band.

"Samuel!" Mom seems surprised to see him. "You're supposed to be downstairs."

Samuel . . . Samuel Gravlox! The name on the radio. . . . That was the band my mom played in . . .

. . . in 1937. She played flute in the Samuel Gravlox Orchestra. Dad and I saw it in an old newspaper that was spit out of the time sphere, right around when the cap showed up. That's how we knew she was back here. I wonder if she was ever on the radio, too.

"We have serious trouble tonight. There is a report that the project—" He stops when he sees me. "Who's this?" It's not a friendly question.

The radio fills the brief silence. "Now, the closing theme to *One Man's Family,* 'Destiny's Dream,' led by guest conductor Elliot Stubin."

"How did he get in here?" Gravlox demands. From his tone of voice, it seems like he's already decided not to like me.

"He's . . ." Now Mom gives me her we're-gonna-keep-a-secret look. I guess knowing all the looks on your family's faces is like having a decoder badge, too.

"He's one of the students in the school here," Mom explains. "His parents are . . . caught in a blizzard, and . . . their train is delayed. He's staying with me." I notice she kind of casually moves her coat over the drawings of me on the table.

"Christmas Eve is a terrible time to go around getting involved with strangers. At least, this particular Christmas Eve."

"He's not a stranger, Samuel."

"Well, you'd better be sure. They sent a spy."

"What? Who?"

"The Nazis, of course. It's no secret they'd love to know what we're up to." He keeps staring at me. "Apparently it's a young spy. Where did you say you're from?" He switches so suddenly to addressing me that it catches me off guard.

Which might be what he wants.

"I . . . I didn't."

"What's your name, young man?"

"Eli Sa, sir." I guess me and Mom have to pretend we're not related.

"So, Eli, where'd you get such funny clothes?"

"Samuel!"

Mom is getting mad at him, but he's not listening. Not to us. He's turned toward the radio. A look of pain crosses his face.

"That damn Stubin! He doesn't know what to do with a baton! Listen to how mushy that passage is! The notes are all running together like molasses! If keeping that orchestra in line were my only job, I'd be going crazy. Well, come on, get your coat."

"Why?" Mom asks.

"Because we've been called in for an emergency briefing. They're worried there's a chance of—" Then his eyes narrow, and he looks at me again. "Where did you say he was from?"

"Valley of the Moon, near Sonoma," I tell him, a little indignantly.

"Well, that's close. There shouldn't be any blizzards there," he says to my mom. "This boy's parents should be here anytime. Anyway, get your things on and meet me downstairs. They've sent a car for us."

He heads for the door. "I'm going downstairs to read Stubin a little of the riot act. But don't meet me in the Venetian Room. It's too public. Meet me around the side entrance. I don't want the whole band to know."

"Isn't it a little too late, Samuel? The way you came up here, and with all this shouting?"

"The Nazis can know that we're on to them. I don't mind that." *I* mind that Gravlox shot me another look when he said that. Can't Mom just tell him who I am? "But we don't have to let the world know what we're going to do about it. I haven't told any of the others. They just want both of us out there, first. Dan doesn't know, either."

"Dan?" Mom suddenly looks a little pale.

"You don't mind?"

"Why should I?" she says.

"Just asking. See you downstairs. Are you sure you trust this boy?" He points right at me.

"Absolutely."

Gravlox faces me again. I guess that's better than having him talk about me like I'm not even here. "There's a war on, young man. We're all in on it. There's no such thing as 'too careful' anymore. Tell that to your parents when they get here." Then he pauses, and with his back to me says, "On second thought, don't tell them anything." He closes the door, and his steps fade away on the hotel carpet.

"It's a little too late for that," I say quietly. "You're not really going with him, are you?"

"Eli . . . I have to."

"Why?"

I can see her thinking about what she's going to say next. "Samuel knows I'm from another time." She reaches for her coat.

"He does?"

"It was his lab I . . . fell into. I collapsed into it, out of the time stream, after being exploded out of the laboratory your father and I had. Samuel's a mathematician at the university across the bay, in Berkeley. He's working on time travel, too. He created a crude device . . . based on atom splitting."

"But, Mom, they don't time-travel now. It's not invented yet."

"I know." She's putting on her scarf.

"I mean, Dad barely has it invented in our own time."

"I know." A mitten slides onto her hand.

"So then why do you have to go to this meeting? And why is somebody spying on a bunch of musicians?"

"Because, hon, the band is just a cover. For quite a few of us."

Now I'm confused. I thought I was going to have some cocoa with my mom, then take her home. "So what is it you really do?" I ask. "Is it the teaching?"

"Samuel helped get me that job, too. I teach art, of all things." She lets a quick smile break out. Now that she's taken her coat, the drawings of me are exposed again on the table. "But that's not what Samuel was here about," she adds.

"So what was it?"

"He thinks I'm working with him and a team of other scientists to help perfect his time-travel device, so he can use it to help the Allies win the war against Germany and Japan."

"Are you?"

"I'm not sure." I get another kiss. "I'll tell

you everything when I get back. Stay right here. Listen to the radio. Take a nap. Order room service if you want to. But do not leave this room—not even to go downstairs. And merry Christmas, Eli. I love you."

"I love you, too. Even if no one's supposed to know I'm you're son."

"No, they're not. If Samuel thought there was another time traveler here, his hair would turn even whiter. And they might not let you go home, either. Bye-bye, sweetie." She heads for the door but turns around to look at me again before she leaves. "I really can't believe you're here." The door closes, and now her footsteps fade away, too.

I'm alone on Christmas Eve, sixty-six years before I was born.

Where's that cocoa?

I start looking around on what I guess are Mom's kitchen shelves—small planks of wood near her sink—but all I see are Saltines, a half-eaten loaf of sourdough bread, a little block of cheese, and a tin of coffee.

I guess finding rice milk to heat up with the Ovaltine is out of the question.

That's when I notice the present. Again.

Mom left it on the table, near the drawings. It's wrapped in green paper, with a bright red ribbon; and her name, written in ink that's bright red, too, is on a little white tag: *Margarite.*

I wonder who it's from.

She's had a whole different life here these last five years, one I don't know anything about.

Who does she celebrate Christmas with now?

A little corner of the package is ripped, and I can see something that looks like . . .

It is. A picture. Not a changing digital display, but a single, flat picture in a frame. One of those old photos.

But like the "antique" chair, this one isn't old yet, either. I pick it up and hold it near the light. It looks like Mom's face inside. Maybe I can see a little more of it if I pull the paper and peek. . . .

It's ripped. I tore the wrapping. Well, since I'm gonna have to retape it anyway, I might as well see. . . .

It's Mom, all right. With some man. She's in the orchestra, standing up, sharing a duet with a guy in a suit, with slicked-back hair. She's on her flute, and he's playing some kind of jumbo clarinet. The whole thing might not be such a big deal, except that the photo is signed: *Here's to more great music together! Dan the Oboe Man.*

Dan the Oboe Man. Dan the *Oboe* Man.

There's an envelope stuck in the frame. On the outside, in the same handwriting as the inscription on the photo, is another note: *I'm playing chamber music. Meet me there. I'll send a car. It'll be fun.*

Oh, *will* it?

Inside is a fancy invitation to some kind of art show:

A Christmas Eve benefit at the de Young,
for the museum and for war bonds!

You're invited to preview the new exhibit,
"Myths, Legends, & Truths:
Fantastic Objects from History."
A festive night with an ancient Yuletide theme!

Merry flippin' Christmas. This guy wants a date with my mom.

Then something else occurs to me: How do I know he hasn't already had one?

I forget all about the Ovaltine.

A few minutes later, the phone starts to ring. It takes me a little while to figure out that it is a phone—the ringing seems too loud, and it's coming from this small-but-heavy appliance on the table by the bed. Plus it's wired to the wall. Then I remember that phone Dad and I saw in the motel in Vinita, Oklahoma, the one he thought belonged in some kind of museum. This lunky thing is a lot like that one.

Maybe it's Mom.

"Hello?"

There's a muffled reply. I'm speaking into

the wrong end. I turn the hand piece around. “Hello?”

“Ma’am?”

“Who’s this?” I don’t sound like a ma’am, and I’m not in the mood for anyone to play jokes on me on some olden-day Christmas Eve when I’m trying to figure out if my mom has a secret life.

“This is the front desk. Is Margarite Franchon there?”

Franchon? That’s her unmarried name.

“I can take a message.”

“Please let her know her car is ready.”

“What car?”

“Her cab. The driver is here to take Miss Franchon to the museum.”

Miss?

“Ma’am?”

I don’t reply to that.

“Did you get the message?”

I got it all right.

I slam down the phone.

Oh, yeah, I got it. My mom's head got all screwed up in the time blast that sent her back here, and she's not sure who she is. She's not sure what's real.

The picture she drew of me, of what I might look like at fifteen, is staring back at me, next to the photo of her and Dan the Oboe Man.

I'm not sure what's real anymore, either.

But I'm gonna go downstairs to find out.

Chapter Three

Thea: My New School

10,271 S.E. (Second Epoch, Saurian Time)

It's quite a magical night here on Saurius Prime. It reminds me of one of our festival nights in Alexandria — perhaps a summer celebration of a lunar eclipse, with lanterns in the streets and people wandering the boulevards with cups of spiced wine or lemon juice sweetened with honey.

Mother would let me stay up very late on such nights. I miss her so much. But I carry her here in my heart.

And I am quite far from Alexandria, while Alexandria is quite far from being able to celebrate anything in her streets. The last time I saw those streets, they were on fire. I escaped with my two time-traveling friends, Eli, from Earth's future, and K'lion, the lizard man—"dinosaur" in Eli's language—whose home is here on this planet, Saurius Prime.

I'm not sure where in the cosmos we are. I've tried to map it out with the telescopes that have been provided for me, and though I seem to recognize many of the constellations, I wonder if it's a trick of my eyes. Or my emotions. This can't be Earth.

Can it?

Soon, however, I plan to get back to more familiar night skies.

"Thea-chick?"

It's Gandy. She looks after me now. She's a bit rounder than K'lion, and older. She wears two circular lenses in front of her eyes—she calls them simply "glasses"—to help her see, and she clucks over me like an aunt. Which is sweet, as Mother had no siblings, and I never had an aunt. Especially not one the size of a small tree. Her skin is the most marvelous speckled green and blue.

"Thea?"

"I'm writing in my journal, Gandy. Another moment."

"You are always writing, nest-*T-TT-TT*-ling."

The Saurians have been gracious—and curious—enough to learn my tongue and speak it to me, even though they can't help but add sounds and ticks of their own. But I'm glad, for I doubt I shall ever learn to speak Saurian.

"I'm a scientist, Gandy. I keep records." I am apparently a curiosity, too—a mammal who has evolved to sentient form. The Saurians still scarcely believe it, since their experience of mammals until now has been one of trying not to step on the small furry creatures who scamper underfoot here on this humid jungle planet of theirs.

"Yes, moonleaf, but surely there can't—*tk!*—be many other mammals who *read*?"

I would remind her that it was the Saurian

Science Academy who asked me to keep a record of my experiences here. They've been studying me, and I've been studying them, writing in these fresh scrolls that they've generously provided. Though the words *writing* and *scrolls* may not be quite accurate.

The "scrolls" are long, gossamer sheets with thin filaments running through them, similar, they tell me, to the apparatus provided to K'lion to record his schoolwork while on his journey.

There is a stylus you can use for the traditional type of writing that I, of course, am used to.

However, the stylus can also keep a record of one's voice and translate it immediately into writing on the scroll sheet itself. Mine comes with what they call a "lingo-spot" so that my scroll may understand me.

But no matter how strange the devices provided to me by the Saurians, I suspect *I* strike them as stranger still. How could it be otherwise?

Gandy, though, does use the Saurian endearment "moonleaf" with me, and has always made sure I've had warm bedding at night and plenty to eat. The Saurians are especially enamored of a stew made, I gather, from some of those scurrying mammals native to this planet, wrapped in broad green leaves and served hot. I've yet to develop a taste for it.

But they have fed me in other ways: When K'lion sent me here in his time-vessel, he was able to rescue several scrolls from the flames of the library at Alexandria—where my mother, Hypatia, was the head librarian and principal lecturer. She was killed by a bloodthirsty mob, followers of a man named Brother Tiberius. He was a monk who feared the unauthorized knowledge to be found in our library. It was his fear that filled him with so much rage.

Tiberius wanted to tell people what and how to think. Perhaps with the library gone he will have an easier time of it.

Here on Saurius Prime, though, they're avidly working on translating every manuscript sent back with me—one on pyramid building was a particular favorite. Each work is added to the library at K'lion's school—the Middle Academy of Applied Science and Cognitive Order, where they've given me my own quarters for study and research. All they ask is that I allow classes to come in occasionally and observe me.

The Saurians fancy themselves as very logical and professionally curious.

"Well, dear chick, *kk-kk-kh!* I've been sent here to inform you that the players *sk-tkt!* are nervous, and they want your help for one more rehearsal. They want *t-t-kh!* everything to be perfect for you."

They're very generous, these Saurians. I keep telling them things don't have to be perfect. Just lively.

They're performing a play that was in the stack of scrolls K'lion saved. It's an old one, composed a few hundred years before I was born, by the Greek writer Aristophanes. Called *The Ditch Diggers,* it's a comedy about men who dig the ditches to bury all the dead left behind in war. Then the diggers get the idea to start burying the men—the generals and leaders—who are causing the war. *Then* the ditch diggers become leaders themselves and start their own war.

It's quite funny.

They won't be performing it in its original Greek, but in Saurian instead. I'll be listening with the help of another of these lingo-spots: Like the scrolls, it is made with technology they call "plasmechanical," which is half biology and half machinery.

The lingo-spot rests behind the ear and manages to insinuate itself into one's skin, one's consciousness, allowing the wearer to "hear" a new language in his or her own words. I'm still not completely sure how it works, and though I use it, I find it a somewhat uncanny invention.

But the reason they're performing *The Ditch Diggers* in the school auditorium is quite touching: It's all part of a farewell celebration held in my honor tonight.

Thea: 10.271 S.E. (Second Epoch, Saurian Time)

I'm scheduled to leave at dawn, in a new kind of time-vessel they've built. Somewhat at my insistence, I am being sent back to the Earth I come from. I want to make contact with Eli. But more important for the Saurians, I'm supposed to find out what happened to K'lion.

Chapter Four

Clyne: Lab Visit

2019 C.E. November

My friend Eli the boy is already gone. And now there's fighting in his nest-house.

I am on the roof, and know I shouldn't be here. I am doing what they call "spying"—watching and listening to somebody, or a lot of somebodies, without them knowing it. It's a skill I have picked up here on Earth Orange, during the time I've spent as an "outlaw."

Before becoming an outlaw, I was, of course, merely a middle school student en route to study one of the more familiar, parallel, Saurian Earths, as required by science class. But I was knocked from the charted time paths by Eli, and later Thea, and I now seem no closer to completing my course work than Saurius Prime is to its moon. On our planet, it was the renegade herbivore philosopher Melonokus who said, "Only an eggshell is predictable, but everything inside and out is subject to scrambling."

I'm beginning to feel scrambled.

Yes, I know I wasn't supposed to read Melonokus's work until I was older.

In my current situation, I am simply trying to record as much as I can of my experiences, and I hope that a detailed record of my time here will make up for much of my missed class work. I have even taken to using their Earth calendar to date my entries, as events tend to happen fast here, and I am attempting to calibrate chronology in the native way to keep track of them all.

Regardless of the dating system used, however, I've had a lot of free time as an outlaw, since my main occupations have been hiding and looking for food. I found myself doing what many of the jobless and neglected sentient mammals do in this culture: I "Dumpster-dive," which is to say, I have learned how to forage for food and supplies in what is often considered waste.

With some of my newfound time, I've been able to tinker with the lingo-spot to record events, or at least my telling of them, which can be done with the barest whisper from me.

To some degree, it justifies talking to myself, which is good, since I've been alone here. Now, though, if I don't speak up, I may be drowned out by the shouting below, which is giving me cranial reverberations. Eli the boy's nest-sire, Sandusky, is arguing with Mr. Howe, who always seems to misunderstand the nature of things.

And yet, despite this ability—or is it an anti-ability?—Mr. Howe appears to work for the central authorities, whose security forces are looking for me.

Mr. Howe is monitoring the progress that

Sandusky the nest-"dad" (*dad* is peculiar mammalian shorthand for "sire," but it pops off the tongue nicely) is making with his own time-vessel.

Dad. I just like saying it. Certain Earth Orange words are like fizzy bubbles on your flavor nodes. *Jazz.* That's another one. *Howdy.* They have much interesting language here.

As for this vessel, that might be too ambitious a description. It's not an object that moves or goes anywhere on its own, but simply a "time sphere." The idea behind it is similar to Melonokus's saying about the stages we pass through while young: "Your shell cracks, and the universe changes." This sphere seems to be more of a crack, or a tear, in the fabric of time, one that Sandusky created in his laboratory. I believe it was an accident—at least the severity and extent of the rip suggest so.

Eli was exposed to some of the energy released by the accident, and the atomic structure of his body seems to have changed, making him able to traverse the Fifth Dimension *by himself,* without an actual vessel. My skin gets all tar-pitty just thinking about it. Imagine the oral reports he could deliver at school!

Below me, they're still arguing about the power residing in the body of this young mammal. In some ways, I may be one of the causes of the current situation.

"It wasn't an accident, Sands! You let him go on purpose. You sent him. You don't have any authority to send him on missions. I mean, my God, World War Two!"

"I'm his father. I know that doesn't count for much in your book, but do you think I would knowingly let him go back there?"

I'm crouched next to a roof window—like a small piece of hothouse glass that lets light in during daytime—and can hear their voices coming up from below. This is a bad place for me to hide, but at least it's dark now. My understanding of the rituals of some of Earth Orange's most famous outlaws, however, is that they would often return to the scenes of their crimes, perhaps in order to be caught.

But even though I have no desire to be famous, like a group elder or a top-stomper in Cacklaw, I would return to the lab when I was supposed to be hiding, and leave things for my friends.

I was careful. I left items in places where I knew only Eli or "Dad" (My taste nodes again! Have I mentioned the word *taco* yet?) would find them. Mostly, I took bits and pieces of things I found in those Dumpsters, and I was able to fabricate a crude version of the time compasses we use in our vessels. If the mammals on Earth Orange were going to start shredding the fabric of time, it seemed best to give them the means of controlling themselves, too. Or at least point them in the right direction.

You'd be amazed what gets thrown away here. I've found computing machines, silicon chips, fluorescent tubing, simple electric engines, medical supplies, pieces of dwellings, various transportation devices, chemicals, paints and sprays, clothes, toys, and plenty of food.

For the compass, though, all I needed was the copper wiring from one of the engines and a collection of highly polished sea stones.

To those I added a battery, then ran the wire around the rocks, setting up a series of "stops" and "starts" for the electric impulse, to mimic crudely what is supposed to happen to light in the simplest of chrono-compasses. The stops and starts are like the basic *ones* and *zeroes* in simple computing devices, and I knew that Sandusky-sire's knowledge would lead him in the right direction to fashion a prototype.

Just to make sure they knew it was from me, I'd leave a sign. I find oranges one of the sweetest gifts of their planet, and would place one next to my offering.

The last time I visited the lab, there was an orange waiting for me, stuffed into the crevice of a nearby tree. There was a query written on it, in their language: *Thanks, but how do I turn it off?*

I'm not sure if that message was from Eli or his father. I didn't have time to find out;

one of the shell-protectors posted by the central authorities was making his rounds, and I barely got away. *Somebody* has been getting glimpses of me, though. In one of the Dumpsters, I found a news tally, a paper one, printed on tree fiber—such an extravagant use of a tree!—called the *National Weekly Truth.* The headline read: DINO-MAN OF THE WOODS? There was a crude rendering next to it that looked vaguely like me.

The snout was much too long, though, and the eyes too close together and dull.

Still, it would seem that outlaws are sometimes famous in spite of themselves. As the saying goes, "All the eggs look the same, but some hatchlings make more noise." Not only was I scrambled, I was getting noisier.

This time, instead of a quick stop, I thought of climbing to the roof. If I could tap on the hothouse window and get Eli the boy's attention, I could actually talk to him. We hadn't spoken since Howe and his corps of shell-protectors tried to corner us at Wolf House.

That's when Thea escaped in my time-vessel and I fled into the woods.

When I arrived at the lab, the squabble-roars between Howe and Sandusky-sire had already erupted. I pieced together that I had missed my friend Eli again: He'd gone back through the Fifth Dimension to find his nest-mother, who herself had become displaced in time due to an earlier lab accident.

"You told me he agreed to let you keep that hat under lock and key! That you'd talked him out of using it by himself! I should have seized it! It's a national-security asset!" Howe's face gets damp and purple like a horned Saurian when he stays angry too long.

"It's a boy's baseball cap," Sandusky-sire says. "And you wanted me to keep testing his reactions to the particle charge. Anyway, I thought he had agreed to let me keep it locked up." Eli's dad isn't squabble-roaring at all now. "He'd become obsessed with the note his mother sent."

"WHY WON'T ANYONE SHOW ME THIS

NOTE!?" It was, apparently, a subject that caused Mr. Howe much agitation, among the many subjects that prompted such a response in him. A night-faring bird fluttered away, itself agitated by the noise from Mr. Howe.

"He took it with him. It was written on Fairmont Hotel letterhead," Sandusky-sire adds. "It was dated 1941. She's been back there a long time."

"That's the year we entered World War Two," Howe says, looking a bit more scared than a moment ago. "We can't have your boy back there changing things around."

"Why not? Maybe so many families won't be blasted apart this time. The way I've lost mine."

Howe doesn't respond to that. Not directly. "Why did Eli think he could even find her back there?"

Sandusky-sire doesn't say anything about the chrono-compass. I wonder if he perfected it. I wonder if he discovered the quantum trace-prints of matter yet, as a way of pinpointing times, beings, and places.

"I was wrong to have been so lax." Howe remains unquiet. "You should have told me about the note immediately. I shouldn't have to hear these things from agents. I'm having you watched twenty-four hours a day now, Sands. We needed that boy for new missions. World War Two is already fought and done with."

"Is that why you came here tonight? To send my son on an errand of your own?"

"No. No." Howe becomes a little distracted, like he'd lost something in his pockets. "I came here because I really *am* having you watched, but not just with guards. We've been planning this for a while anyway—I didn't realize how necessary it had become."

"More surveillance?" Sandusky-sire sounds like he doesn't much care. "You already know I don't say anything important into any of my phones or Comnet devices."

"Yes, well, speaking of Comnet, we've

launched a couple of new satellites," Howe says, damp and minimally purple. "We've trained one of them here on Moonglow, your lab, and the area around it. It monitors large, moving masses. Nothing can really hide from it. Everyone authorized to be in the zone will have their own transmitter. Here." He holds out what looks to be a kind of lingo-spot to Eli's father.

"A leash. I'm not wearing it."

"I'm afraid you'll have to. If you want to enter or leave the zone. Stay inside the lab, though," Howe says with a shrug, "and suit yourself."

"How nice that I have a choice."

"Well, that's just it. We want you to think of this as something that protects you. And will protect Eli, when he returns. It will all be complete when the final link is turned on." Howe now holds out a small control pad to Sandusky-sire, who won't take it. "I thought I would come over and make a celebration of it."

"Yippee." It's not a happy sound.

"I would've thought you'd like the extra security, given the high-level work you're doing here."

"I'll feel secure when my family's together, Howe. And when you leave us alone."

"Well, we'll see what we can do about the 'left alone' part." Howe takes the controls and pushes one with his thumb. "There, that signal turns on the link to the satellite, which should already be focused—"

But he doesn't finish the sentence. I experience immediate tympanic distress as alarms go off, while a bright light explodes overhead, like a small sun going supernova.

"What's that!?" Sandusky-sire yells.

"That," Howe shouts back, "is what happens when there's an intruder!"

I leap away, hoping not to be discovered. But I don't get far at all before I hear the whirring motors of flying machines coming in my direction.

Chapter Five

Eli: Po

December 24, 1941 C.E.

"You Dan?"

The cab driver looks up at me. I guess not. He doesn't match the picture.

"No, I'm Dang." He draws out the *g*. "Charlie Dang. You're not"—he looks down at a slip of paper—"Margarite?"

"I'm her . . . one of her students. I'm Eli."

"Well, I'm supposed to take her"—another glance at the paper—"to Golden Gate Park."

"*What?*" I didn't like the sound of that. "Why would she want to go to the park?"

"To the museum there. The de Young. For the fundraiser. The party, you know." He gives me a quizzical look. "Why do you care what your teacher is doing on Christmas Eve? Where are your parents?"

"They're . . . out of town. She's looking after me. Wants me to meet her there."

I stand there, shivering. An actor from *One Man's Family* strolls out of the hotel, smoking a pipe and waving at someone across the street.

"So you getting in or what?" It's cold, and I don't know what else to do, so I slide in the back. "I'm confused, kid. So this Margarite isn't coming?"

"No. I'll catch up with her."

"All right." Charlie Dang throws the car in gear. "A kid oughtta be with his family on Christmas Eve, though. Are your parents gone because of something to do with the war?" He's looking at me in the rear-view mirror.

"Pretty much."

We drive through the fog awhile, and I don't feel like talking. What am I supposed to say, really? That neither I nor my parents have even been born yet, and I've come back in time almost eighty years to try and find my mom?

We're stopped at a red light. I hear the clanging of what must be a cable car, but I can't see anything in the mist.

"Po."

He says it so suddenly, I almost jump out of the seat.

"What?"

"Po." The cab is moving again, almost gliding, since we can't see anything around us, and Charlie Dang is pointing out the window. "On nights like these, I always think they're out there."

"Who's out there?"

"*Po.* In Hawaii, where I grew up, *po* was the underworld. But in China, where my parents are from, *po* are souls. Spirits. And sometimes those spirits turn into Marchers of the Night, or tapping ghosts."

"Tapping ghosts?" I must have sounded surprised—they have tapping ghosts in Barnstormer games. How did he know? You use them for pinch-hitting. Mostly bunts.

"Tapping ghosts are folk who won't stay buried. Something bad happened to them, and they just can't rest."

Again, just like Barnstormers. The monsters on your team can't stop. They have to move on to the next town, to the next game, before they're caught. And once more, I'm starting to feel that way, too.

I haven't had a normal conversation with anyone since Dad and I drove to California in our truck. And with my mom already gone, even that wasn't too normal.

I start telling Charlie everything about Barnstormers, how these monsters play pickup games in local towns for food and money. I tell him everything except the part about playing it over the Comnet. The rest just spills out of me, like I'm talking to some new kid at school.

"And it's set way back in time, too, like the 1930s!"

"Way back, huh? Two whole years ago!" Charlie's laughing, "Never knew baseball could be so scary. I like those Seals, though!" He jerks his thumb at my cap. "They used to come and train in Hawaii, in a town called Hana. You ever hear of Hana?"

I've heard of Hawaii.

"Guy who owns 'em owns a sugar plantation there. On the island of Maui! Lotta free baseball in the spring. We stand around and watch. Saw DiMaggio there! Hey, he's supposed to be here tonight, I think."

The cab rolls to a stop.

DiMaggio?

I look up, and there are rows of lanterns overhead, more bright lights, and people moving past my window in heavy overcoats and hats.

We're at the museum.

"We're here, kid. Happy holidays. Hope your parents stay safe. Have a good party."

I step out.

"Forty cents."

"Did you say Joe DiMaggio is going to be here?"

"Yeah, that's what I heard. Cabbies hear things all the time, though." I hand him a dollar and he glances at it—then the glance turns into a stare.

Right. I just goofed. The money's not from here. From this time. But that's not what he says.

"Po," he whispers. "All over the place tonight. Watch out." Then he winks at me and drives off.

There are a bunch of people on the steps, waiting to get their invitations checked so they can get inside. I reach into my pocket for the one this Dan guy sent my mom . . . and it's not there. It's not *there*! I thought I stuffed it in my pocket.

Now how am I going to get in?

I stand with everybody on the museum steps. There's a Santa Claus ringing a bell wishing everyone a very merry Christmas.

Next to Santa is a man with a heavy gray overcoat and a hat, putting out a cigarette. DiMaggio dressed like that, and I think he did cigarette ads, too. I saw one, just a picture from an old paper magazine, somewhere on the Comnet.

I guess in those days—these days—there were still a lot of places you could smoke in public. But why'd he need to do the ad at all? He was already a Yankee. Didn't they pay him enough?

"Mr. DiMaggio?" Even if I don't get in, I want to meet him.

The man laughs. He raises his head, and as the hat's shadow lifts, I can see it isn't DiMaggio at all.

"Do I look like Joltin' Joe, kid? I guess I'm flattered. But my name's Caen." He sticks out his hand. "Herb Caen. DiMaggio probably won't come. He hates these dog-and-pony shows for the swells. I gotta go inside, though. See how the beautiful people of Baghdad-by-the-Bay try to make it through this war."

"What do you mean, 'Baghdad'?" The fog still hadn't lifted, and after Charlie Dang's *po* talk, I'm feeling a little strange. And maybe, out here all alone, a little scared.

This *is* still San Francisco, right?

Caen laughs. "The Baghdad thing's just a nickname I coined for our sweet little burg. In my job, I go back and forth between telling the absolute truth and making things sound a little better than they really are."

"What job is that?" It's like I'm walking into a setup for a joke.

"I'm a newspaper columnist. *San Francisco Chronicle.* You read it?"

"Online." Oops.

"Yeah, I read it in line myself, sometimes. When I have to. Well, happy Yuletide, and hopefully this war will be over before you hit draft age."

He tips his hat and is about to leave, but stops and peers around. "Hey. Who are you here with, kid? Where are your folks?"

"They're . . . I'm supposed to meet them

inside." I shrug. I guess I don't have to pretend my mom's really my teacher if he doesn't know who she is. "But I lost my ticket."

That's not quite a lie. And anyway, after my "online" slip-up, does he really want to hear that my parents technically don't even exist yet?

"We'll tell 'em you're with me. Come on. A kid shouldn't be alone on Christmas Eve."

Yeah, right.

His plan works. We go in, and it looks almost . . . *magical* inside. The whole museum's decked out with Christmas decorations. There are candles and ornaments around all the displays, and a pair of musicians is playing in the corner. It's all very festive.

"I don't think the fact we're at war has sunk in yet," Caen says. "Well, kid, enjoy yourself while you can." He grabs a drink from a waiter and walks into the crowd.

A huge banner says MYTHS, LEGENDS, & TRUTHS: FANTASTIC OBJECTS FROM HISTORY. There's a "Haunted California" area, a "Mysteries of the East" display (I wonder if they have anything about *po*), but I'm closest to the "King Arthur's Round Table" area, where the first thing I see is a large pair of white antlers in a display case.

Next to that is something that I recognize from my childhood: the Dino Sword.

But before I can even take a step toward it, some big kid with slick blond hair and a too-large suit plows into me and knocks me over.

Chapter Six

Thea: Plasmechanical Dawn

10,271 S.E.

The play was a success. All the Saurians appear to have enjoyed it, which they signified by stomping their large feet on the floor, or in some cases slapping their tails. I wonder if they understood it, though. From what I can tell of their history, they haven't actually had a war in a very long time.

They do, however, have Cacklaw, their ritual sporting event, which *looks* somewhat like a war at times. This is especially true during the period known as "free reign," where the rules are suspended and alliances change. As far as I can gather, there has only ever been one, long single game of Cacklaw—passed along, generation after generation—knitting the whole culture together throughout its history. It's as much a collection of myths to live by as it is an athletic competition.

There is so much to learn about Cacklaw, about the Saurians, about this planet, its atmosphere, and the nearly familiar constellations in its night sky. I am especially enamored of the star formation they call the Gatherer, which reminds me somewhat of Osiris in our own sky, named for the god who represents hope in times of darkness.

There is much to learn, and I wish someday to have the chance. But right now, the time has come to leave.

The Saurians have been worried about K'lion since he failed to return to class. They have nothing against me particularly—but a mammal who can talk, write, and produce plays will always be peculiar to them.

But still, as Kolomus, who appears to function as a kind of prelate of the city here, told me last night, "You have opened our eyes a little wider."

It was quite a compliment, though I am not sure I warrant it. And it was certainly unlike anything I heard in Alexandria from Brother Tiberius.

Now the heavy-lidded eyes of Kolomus, Gandy, and hundreds of others are open and fixed on me.

They've gathered around in "the reaching field," a place dedicated to the dispatch and return of their journeying time-vessels.

Mine is the only departure they have allowed, or will allow, for a while.

They remain bothered that K'lion may be "stuck" somewhere in one of their histories, undoing or redoing events, which is always to be avoided. Except for the various "sorties" in Cacklaw, as they call each round, or contest, the Saurians like to avoid surprises. K'lion's disappearance has proven too unpredictable for them. They are still trying to understand what went wrong with such a routine class assignment.

In response, they set about changing the essential design of their time-ships, using plasmechanics. Plasmechanics form the basis of lingo-spot technology, which so effectively translates languages between members of different—I was about to say *cultures,* but perhaps *species* is more accurate. Or even *planet-dwellers.*

From what I can gather, plasmechanical devices are machines constructed on the level of the tiniest particles imaginable: living tissue made to "build" more of itself as it adapts to each new wearer, each new language, or in the case of ships, each new situation. Apparently, the Saurians have imbued plasmechanical material with an even greater intelligence than before.

Which raises the question of whether such devices can still properly be considered "machines" at all.

The Saurians seem to be undertaking a great

experiment with self-perpetuating technology. I can only imagine that Mother would be fascinated—and concerned. "The soul of things," she once told me, "is hard to quantify."

The Saurians had observed that left on its own, a plasmechanical device, such as a lingo-spot, would grow and change slightly, like a cell, before eventually becoming less effective. It would burn out and need to be replaced.

Until I arrived.

According to Gennt, a senior minister of engineering, one of the scrolls saved from the library, having to do with mummification, has been of great use.

"Odd things you mammals do with flesh. But useful," he told me. The Saurians were especially fascinated by the use of oils and spices in conserving mummy skin. They found their own planetary equivalents of both myrrh and cinnamon, which were key ingredients in the mixture applied to the bodies. This simple, ancient formula has allowed the Saurians to preserve sheets of plasmechanical material.

Thus they discovered that the nervelike connections that run through the devices could actually continue to grow, and the larger a sheet, or piece, of plasmechanical material, the more easily the machine—if it is still a machine—can begin repairing itself.

Not only repairing itself, but learning, too. Subtly adapting for whatever task is at hand.

So they set about designing a time-vessel to include large plasmechanical components. I'm to use the prototype in the search for K'lion.

The initial plan is to allow the ship to serve as a kind of tracking device. They've given it a "scent," as it were—a bit of K'lion's DNA—which should allow the craft to hone in on him like a hunting dog, if the ship gets anywhere within range.

Of course, no one has actually tested the ship yet. Since K'lion has yet to return, the Saurians worry that the Fifth Dimension has grown unsafe for travelers.

But were there ever guarantees for any journey through time?

"I'd *t-ka!* take it into the field myself," Gennt told me, "but if mammals evolve so *p-p-kh* fast, and Saurians have vanished, maybe the field isn't what it used to be."

By "field," he meant the Fifth Dimension, which allows a voyager basically an infinite number of choices of where—or when—to go. Or sometimes, who to be. The Fifth Dimension can't change, but the travelers that go through it—and the destinations it leads to—always do.

Of course, most travelers don't want infinite choices. They want an adventure, to be changed a little perhaps, then they want to return.

Like me.

So I volunteered to take the time-ship on her maiden voyage.

At first they refused, insisting it would be too dangerous. But I told them the risk was my choice, and besides, K'lion was last seen on my planet. Perhaps it is I, the mammal, who should seek to undo what K'lion's encounter with our species has begun.

Of course, I am not completely sure that such an undoing is possible, but I am willing to try for a chance to return home. Or, given that my home in Alexandria was burned to the ground and my mother murdered, someplace simply familiar and safe.

It's that or live my life now as an explorer. Mother would appreciate that.

Either way, it made sense to volunteer to try out the ship. I promised to send K'lion back home in it if I could.

They have a tradition here of sending off "chronauts,"—a word I've fashioned for their time-explorers—at dawn.

I believe this ritual has something to do with the time of day that the Saurians' original king—the great Temm, who is said to have invented Cacklaw—set off on the journey in which he was to learn the rules of the game.

In any case, I am honored. Gandy, Kolomus, Gennt, and so many others are here. And Gandy is even giving me a *sklaan,* a thin, gossamer-like garment made of special fibers designed to keep the wearer warm in almost any climate.

Of course, originally designed for a Saurian, it's a bit big for me.

"For your journey, moonleaf. Be nourished." Then Gandy hands me a basket filled with leaf jellies and animal purees—Saurian delicacies—for my voyage.

I have never observed a Saurian cry before, but her eyes seem wet.

My eyes are damp, too. After so many months here, I will miss these lizard folk. They have provided me a place to rest, to study, and to heal.

And now, once their second, larger, orange sun rises to complement the smaller white one, I will climb into the plasmechanical ship that awaits me.

And I will take leave of my new friends, to see if once lost, you can ever find anything like home again.

Chapter Seven

Eli: Sword and Oboe

December 24, 1941 C.E.

The Dino Sword. But that's not what it's called here. Here it's called EXCALIBUR! KING ARTHUR'S "DRAGON SWORD," WHICH LET HIM RULE OVER A KINGDOM. And then a smaller sign below that says REPLICA BASED ON HISTORICAL SOURCES.

I'm looking right up at it, from my place on the floor. Up at the sword, the lights, and the big jerk who plowed into me.

I'm a little dizzy. A memory of being about four years old, and watching a cartoon on an early Comnet screen comes floating back. *The Adventures of King Arthur and Laddy.*

Laddy was a sidekick. A little boy, not much older than I was then. Arthur had an enchanted sword, which Laddy would sometimes try to use, getting himself into a jam when he did. Together, the king and Laddy would chase dragons. But the dragons all looked like dinosaurs to me. When Mom would come in the afternoons, after the show was over, I'd sit in her lap and tell about the Dino Sword.

They called it "Dragon Sword" on the show, but I always called it "Dino Sword" instead. And so did Mom.

"You stupid little kid." It's the blond guy who crashed into me. He's not even that much older than me. Maybe around fifteen or so. Maybe he thinks the suit and tie make him look like a hotshot.

And he pronounces *kid* like "kit."

"Hey, *you* crashed into *me*!"

He doesn't respond, doesn't even offer me a hand up, just continues on his way. Which turns out to be straight through the front door.

I'm glad he's gone.

I get up and brush myself off. No one seems to notice. There's a crowd nearby, but they aren't paying much attention to the Dino Sword. They're looking at the exhibit next to it, a pair of white antlers in another display case. The horns are like thick spider webs made of knives—or maybe icicles.

A waiter comes by. "Crepe?"

I don't know what a crepe is, exactly, but I take one so that I'll blend in better. It turns out to be sort of like a folded pancake, or a sweet burrito.

"Thanks. Say, do you know why everyone's crowded around those deer horns? What makes them so special?"

"I don't know, young sir. They're supposed to have some mysterious powers. But that applies to most of the things here. I just hope they have the power to let me earn a little overtime tonight."

He nods and is gone, but not before I take another crepe.

I head over to the antlers. I'm having kind

of a bad night—especially for a Christmas Eve—and I could use a little magic.

"Everyone wants to see the White Stag, kid." I turn around. It's Caen. He's drinking some champagne. "I'd offer you a sip, but I might get in trouble." He winks at me and tilts his glass toward the case. "The de Young is claiming the antlers are real, straight from King Arthur's forest, but they won't tell anyone how they got 'em. Even the British embassy wants to know. The mystery makes 'em more valuable as a fundraising device, I guess. But they're splitting half the money—"

"Don't tell me. With war bonds."

"Right. I guess that's the kind of thing you do when there's a big war on. Maybe I was wrong. Maybe people realize what's happening, after all. Say, you still want to meet DiMaggio?"

"Yeah!" Suddenly I'm feeling a little less gloomy.

"He's over there, near the back. Apparently the Yankee front office thought it would be a swell thing if he came and, you know, spoke a few words about our boys in uniform."

"He'll have to say them pretty loudly." Between the music and the crowd noise, I'm almost shouting myself.

"It's only noisy, kid, because tonight this isn't a museum, it's the 'Last Chance Saloon.'"

"What do you mean?"

"There aren't going to be too many more parties like this for a while. With the war here, people are afraid. That's why everyone's a little extra loud tonight. Keep the ghosts at bay."

I wonder if he knows Charlie Dang.

He finishes his champagne and sets the empty glass down on a display case. Inside is one of the "Haunted California" items—a whip used by an outlaw named Joaquin who became a ghost himself. A headless one, even. According to the sign.

"Spooky stuff, huh?" Caen says. "The replica of his pickled head is right over there." He points around the corner of the case. "At least, they claim it's a replica. Either way, that oughtta cheer everyone up. Say, kid, did your mom and pop ever get here?"

"No, not yet." I look around the room, wondering if my mom is going to find out about this and show up after all.

"Too bad, they'll miss out on Joltin' Joe."

I turn to follow him, when a voice booms across the room: There's a man up near the musicians, talking into one of those giant voice amplifiers like the radio actors were using at the hotel. It's amazing how big all the electronic equipment is back here.

"Hold on to your hat, kid—you're about to get pitched."

"What do you mean, 'pitched'?"

"Our revered host is about to say a few words."

"LADIES AND GENTLEMEN!"

He definitely wanted to be heard above the noise.

"I'M CHESWICK TRIPPLEHORN, THE DIRECTOR OF THE MUSEUM, AND IT'S MY

PLEASURE TO WELCOME YOU TO THE DE YOUNG!"

"Come on," Caen whispered. "Let's sneak over and see Joe before he leaves."

"IT'S A DARK TIME IN THE WORLD, LADIES AND GENTLEMEN! A DARK TIME. WE DIDN'T KNOW HOW DARK WHEN WE CURATED THIS EXHIBITION. BUT NOW THAT THE WORST HAS HAPPENED—WELL, IT CAN ONLY GET BETTER FROM HERE ON!"

There's some applause, and I think—*can it be?*—I see Joe DiMaggio in the back, standing next to a pillar. He has his hands in his pockets, like he's cold.

"SO LET'S WIN THIS WAR FAST, AND LET'S START TONIGHT, WITH A LITTLE IMAGINATION AND MAGIC!"

A little more applause. As we pass the Asian section, I see a whole display about the *po*. After I meet DiMaggio, I'm going to come back and look at it.

"NOW, PLEASE JOIN ME IN THANKING

THE TWO MUSICIANS BEHIND ME, ON LOAN FROM THE SAMUEL GRAVLOX ORCHESTRA—JOHN REESE ON VIOLIN AND DAN STERNING ON THE OBOE!"

I stop dead in my tracks.

Dan Sterning . . . Dan the Oboe Man!

"Hey, kid!" Caen doesn't know why I'm suddenly walking in the other direction, but there's no time to tell him.

Ol' Dan and the violin guy start playing a Christmas carol, the kings one—"We Three Kings of Orient Are"—except there are just two of *them.* I walk right up and grab Dan's oboe and pull it out of his mouth.

"Hey, what's your problem!?"

"Stay away from my mom . . . banshee butt!"

"What?"

He didn't even know he'd been insulted. "Banshee butt" was a name Andy and I came up with to razz each other in Barnstormers. Maybe it came out now because of all the *po*-talk. Or maybe it was dawning on me that everybody in the room—everybody I'd seen—

was already banshee material—ghosts, spirits—by the time I was born. Including this guy who was after my mother.

"What're you . . . What mom?"

"Margarite Sands! My mom hasn't been 'Franchon' since she got married! To my dad!"

"Margarite? She's not married." Dan stares at me. "She would have told me. Are you pretending to be her kid?"

Pretending? That's it. I officially hate this guy. Without thinking about it, I slam the oboe down on the floor.

Out of the corner of my eye, I see a security guard hurrying over. And Herb Caen, too. Oh, great—now I'm gonna be in a newspaper!

The guard grabs me around the waist.

Dan just stands there, blinking. "Margarite . . . Margarite's married?"

"You bet she is!"

"And you're really her . . . ?"

"I'm her kid!" Oh, great, now everybody in 1941's got *me* saying "kid." And I guess I just blew the whole "teacher-student" cover.

"Well, jeez, kid, I never—" He looks around the room. "Where is she?"

"She's with Gravlox! So I guess she's doing a little better in the band than *you* are!"

The guard pulls me away. "It's all right, Mr. Sterning. I'll throw this little runt out."

"Wait a minute. Let me talk to him," says Dan, who just picked up his dented oboe.

He puts his hand on my shoulder to draw me aside, but I jerk away.

"It's possible we have a little misunderstanding here," he says.

"That's one way to put it."

"Did you say Margarite—"

"My mother!"

"Your mother is with Gravlox? Tonight?"

"Yeah."

"But . . ." He looks around, frustrated. "But they're not supposed . . . Did they go to the fort?"

Of course, I don't even know what "the fort" is, but I'm sure as heck not gonna tell this guy.

"What's it to you?" I ask.

He's not just frustrated now, but jumpy. Then he does about the last thing I was expecting: He lifts up his oboe, or what's left of it, and blows, playing what almost sounds like another few bars of "We Three Kings."

Then something happens that's even more unexpected: The lights go out. Now the museum is lit only by candles. It's eerie, but kind of cool. I don't have time to think about it, though, because there's commotion—I hear voices and what sounds like shoving—and then the candles start getting tipped over. It's pitch dark.

Then comes the sound of breaking glass. And screaming.

Chapter Eight

Clyne: Zoo

2019 C.E. November. Monday.

I am in a place they call the zoo. A zoo is supposed to be a collection of different species, "animals" as they say here, which are put on display. But right now I seem to be the only object on view for my human keepers.

They brought me here after capturing me on the roof of Sandusky-sire's lab. I rode in the cold, dark hold of one of their air machines.

Like the animals in a zoo, they have a species name for me, too: Stenonychosaurus.

I looked it up on one of their computing devices. A stenonychosaurus is a type of

Saurian—a "dinosaur"—that used to live on this Earth. Their theory is that I am an evolved version of one. Or more likely, the Earth Orange humans think, I am a "space alien," even though it is they, of course, who live in the far reaches of space and time.

"Are you invading us?" the female known as Thirty asked me.

"Invade? *kkkk . . . taa!*" She had it all wrong. "I simply wish to get back home before the school year is terminated and final marks are handed in."

"This can be like a school, too. We can learn from each other. I want you to trust me." She smiled at me. "I've read the reports of what happened out at the Sandses' lab, with Eli and the girl you were traveling with. I want to help get your friends back."

She wanted to help me, yet she was still called by her number. Thirty. On Saurius Prime, we are numbered only until we leave our community nests to undergo our Passage Calls, in which we get our life-names.

If she didn't qualify for a real name yet, she was probably still much too young to be out by herself. Perhaps she was being given some kind of test, and I should humor her to help her win high marks. "Back from *ting!* where?"

"From wherever they've gone in time. Your friend Eli is supposed to be working for us."

"Who is 'us'?"

"I'm part of the government here. That's all you need to know."

"In truth, young friend, there is much more I would love *sktt!* to know. Can you *k-kk* tell me what happened to the Saurian race here? And can you ascertain, please, whether I am still *pk-pan!* an outlaw?"

"Why do you think you're an outlaw, Mr."—she glanced down at a screen where she appeared to keep some notes—"Klein. That's an Earth name, too. Is it one you picked up here?"

She said it wrong, not quite with a Saurian pronunciation. "Clyne," I corrected her, as gently as I could.

"Klein. Yes." She nodded. "How did you pick that name? Did you meet someone named Klein?"

"Yes, well. I would meet 'Clyne' *tk-bng!* in the Fifth Dimension only if I passed myself *t-t-kh!* coming while I was going. Or versa vice. And that would result from sloppy piloting and deduct points off *pk-pk-pk!* my final marks."

"The Fifth Dimension? Is that how you got here?"

"Why, yes! How else *kt!* could I find an Earth so full of *k-pt-chk!* surprises?"

"Were you trying to surprise us, Mr. Klein?" Here the one called Thirty leaned over to peer at me closely, as if I were a project in science class. "Were you here to arrange a sneak attack?"

"Sneak attack?" It was a type of Earth Orange phrase I hadn't heard before. Then I figured it out. "Oh! *p-p-pw!* A shadow move! Like in Cacklaw!"

Then Thirty appeared to grow very frustrated. She put down her stylus and stopped taking notes. "Like in war, Mr. Klein. When you're done with your games, perhaps we'll talk again.

She exited the room, and I was escorted back to the quarters where they kept me locked up. Why did she get so upset if she knew that Cacklaw was a game? I was actually quite impressed—few mammals on Earth Orange appear to have heard of it.

One time, she and the one called Howe gave me a bio-reconnoiter. I was tied to a table, with my eyes propped open. They poked my hide, clipped off bits of my claws and put them in sample jars, measured my tail, and looked at my tongue.

Apparently Saurian medicine was a mystery to them, and I was their training ground.

"We think," Howe said, "that you *are* a stenonychosaurus. One that evolved to be like us, with two legs for standing upright and a large brain. You would have *been* us, would have kept right on evolving, been this Earth's top species, if that meteor hadn't hit." He was sweating a little bit, and I wasn't sure why he was getting so mad, since I was the one who was restrained and getting prodded. "Do you get angry knowing our kind is in charge here?"

If he meant that he and Thirty were actually the leaders of the humans, it wasn't anger that I was feeling so much as increased nervousness.

"Oh, we know what you are, all right. We just don't know where you're from. Our own past? Another planet? But we'll figure it out. If you're a scout for an invasion, if you came to steal the Earth from us, it won't work. We'll figure it out."

"Stealing *k-k-tu!* is strictly forbidden on *pk!* field trips!" In response, Howe tightened some of the straps to make it more difficult for me to speak.

"Howe, maybe you need to take a few deep breaths. Perhaps he was ready to talk."

"Talk!" Howe bellowed back at Thirty. "He's just playing mind games with us!"

Clyne: 2019 C.E. November. Monday.

Games again! These two Earth Orange mammals had the strangest way of playing!

Howe's face turned a different color, just like the small, four-legged stickleplumes do on Saurius, and he stomped away, letting Thirty take over. "We won't give up, you know," she told me. "Our planet's security is too important. We will eventually accommodate each other. One way or another."

Maybe she was hinting that eventually the games here would actually become fun. But I doubt it.

I am now a "prisoner," which is even more restrictive than being an outlaw. Prisoners are not permitted to play too many games. Aside from that, conditions, under the circumstances, are acceptable: They observe me, feed me oranges when I ask for them—and freshly chopped mammals, even when I don't. Those they serve raw, which they incorrectly assume I like. They have yet to know the wonders of fern-wrapped meat cooked on hot volcanic rocks.

They have also allowed me use of the crude knowledge and communication machine they refer to as "that twenty-year-old piece of junk."

They left some tools. It appeared this was a sneak test, a stealth quiz, the kind you hear about in the upper grades. They wanted to observe me perform a mechanical operation. So I fixed the machine.

That excited them so much they gave me a stack of round flat discs to use, one called a *World Book,* another about dinosaurs, another about constellations. The machine basically reads information off the discs, and they've all been very interested to see what sort of research I can do with such primitive devices.

At times, I am not quite sure if I am a prisoner, after all, or simply here to help them with *their* homework. They seem to be worried about some assignment they can't discuss yet and are constantly whispering about among themselves. Perhaps another sneak test for me? Or are Howe and Thirty being given one by someone else?

I mentioned this was a zoo. I think the humans keep other beings they consider strange, or perhaps even dangerous, here. But unlike the one where Eli and I crash-landed in Alexandria, here the inhabitants are not free to roam about.

I hear them, though, when I'm moved around the grounds—other voices, not all of them human-, or even mammal-, sounding. One time, passing a door, I saw what looked like a large, round black eye peering out at me. But I couldn't be sure. It quickly pulled away from the grate. And I was hurried along.

I've never really seen the other . . . prisoners? Or shall I say classmates? Whoever they are, they keep us all separate. I am taken out of my quarters once a day, into a space called "the yard."

"This place is for you to exercise. To move about. Do you understand?" The guards speak to me in a slow, deliberate cadence, as if I were still young enough to have only a number, too.

"Yes. Can you understand me *skt!* as well?" I thought it was only courteous to make sure.

"Sure, I under—hey, it doesn't matter if *I* understand!"

"It doesn't?"

"I'm supposed to ask *you* the questions!"

I'm not sure what sort of research goes on here, or what kind of quarantine I'm under. But the mammals overseeing this oddly spliced-together institute—zoo-prison-school—are especially prickly and defensive. I wish Eli were here to explain more of his world to me.

Or, perhaps, to explain more of me to his world.

"Go on now, move! This is your fifteen minutes of *fun*! Run! Jump!" The guard prods me with his stick, and I start to move around the yard, taking a couple of flying leaps just to keep my hind-hoppers tuned up.

During yard breaks, I also get to record notes like this into the altered lingo-spot. I hope eventually I can transfer these remarks to the proper forms and worksheets, so I can present this adventure as legitimate classwork.

"Move along!" The guard doesn't like me to slow down. I believe he considers it a kind of resistance.

I jump some more, hopping from one ray of sunlight to another, making a small game of it for myself, imagining I'm working my way—with medium acceleration—through a fallen grid in Cacklaw. There's a dome over most of the complex here. I flew over it, watching from the net that carried me under their roto-spinning flying machines, and could see that it's designed to look like part of the surrounding hills to the world outside. Despite the camouflage, a few sections are crafted to let in true sunlight, which they use to help warm the area. Like a greenhouse, the dome keeps some of the heat from escaping.

I'm jumping faster now, leaping across the yard, clearing several beams of sunlight at once. If I ever do get back, I may not become a top-stomper in Cacklaw, but with practice, I could be a proficient midstepper.

I'm midstepping and bounding now, and extra guards have started to appear in the yard, standing around nervously with their hands on what I believe to be some kind of blasters. Apparently if I move either too slow or too fast, it's cause for alarm.

As I stomp, a quick shadow flickers by, like that made by a small winged Saurian, or one of the avian creatures here.

But there's nothing in the yard.

Then I see another shadow flickering past the sunbeams. This time, though, it doesn't go away. It grows.

And it's accompanied by a familiar humming music that sounds . . . like home. Perhaps an ancient harvest song—a chorus—that the gatherers would sing when they were out in the old forests, collecting mossy greens.

The music grows louder. I stop practicing any kind of a midstep, and the guards unsheath their blasters. The shadow now covers the whole skylight—and crashes through it.

Glass and metal rain down on us, and a ship, a very Saurian-looking ship, lowers itself into the yard.

Alarms make their screech-waves, and blasters flash like small, frantic volcanoes. Looking up at the barred windows that ring the yard, I could almost swear by old Temm himself I see that strange, large, black eye peeping through one of the slits, before it vanishes again.

But I don't have time to think about it very long.

Shots bounce off the ship, which lowers itself steadily toward me. Has another student come searching for me, to claim *extra* extra credit for bringing me back?

More guards pour into the yard. Thirty is with them.

They're rolling out a large type of cannon, with coils around it. They're very fond of particle and laser weapons on this planet, so perhaps it is a primitive destabilizer ray of some sort.

I try to stay out of blast range as the door to the ship slides open. If the guards land a shot inside, it will be a glum welcome for whoever is piloting.

But I suppose one can't stay out of the line of fire forever. I aim for the vessel, going for the kind of jump a top-stomper could be proud of.

The ship is too high. I miss.

Landing hard on the ground, I roll over. I don't get another chance to jump before the particle beam fires. Astonishingly, when it hits the ship, the vessel wobbles but seems to . . . absorb the energy.

All the guards, and Thirty, stand still for a moment, wondering what's just gone wrong. In that pause, I top-stomp again, just make the open ledge of the ship, holding on with my foreclaws.

"K'lion?"

A mammal voice I know. It's Thea. She

doesn't pronounce my name quite right, either, but I don't mind.

"But how did you—?" we ask each other at the same moment.

There's no time for an answer, of course. I pull myself in and the hatch slam-cracks shut behind me. Thea then makes one of the most stomper-like piloting moves I've ever witnessed: She tilts the ship vertically and shoots it out of the gap in the top of the dome before the zoo staff can regroup and start firing again.

"I don't believe—" Once again, we speak simultaneously. There's so much to say, we can only start by lapsing into silence.

Chapter Nine

Eli: Yankee Clipper

December 24, 1941 C.E.

"To tell you the truth, kid, in the off-season I try to avoid crowds." That's Joe DiMaggio, and he's actually talking to me.

We're standing outside the de Young, and the police are trying to interview everybody. The antlers are gone. When the lights went out, somebody stole the White Stag's horns. So far nobody's been able to tell the police anything—no one saw who it was. When the cops get to me, I might just tell them it was Dan the Oboe Man, on general principles. I notice he managed to slip away, too, so why not?

A lot of people are shivering in their tuxedos and evening gowns. They're anxious for the cops to hurry up and let them back in for their coats.

I'm cold, too, but I'm not in any rush. After all, I'm standing next to a real live, famous, dead baseball player. In his pre-dead days, of course.

"When you shut that music fella up, you did me a favor," DiMaggio cracked when I finally met him a few minutes ago. It was dark, but the glow from his cigarette let me see his face. He was trying to stand as far away from the street lamps and the hanging lanterns around the museum as he could. "I didn't want to give a big speech."

"How come?"

"It wouldn't be *me* doing it, it'd be 'Joltin' Joe,' 'the Yankee Clipper.' See? Me, I really don't have anything in particular to say."

"But, you *are* Joltin' Joe."

"Nah, Joltin' Joe's just my disguise now. A

character. If you ever get famous, you'll know. What'd you say your name was again, kid?"

He blew out more smoke, and I coughed. "Sorry. Guess you're too young to puff 'em yourself. Let me get a couple more drags and I'll snuff it out."

I'm standing next to DiMaggio thanks to that reporter, Caen.

I was ushered outside with everybody else after the police got here. I figured maybe my best bet would be to find another cab, hope no one noticed the date on my future money, and go back to the hotel.

But Caen found me first. "Some party, huh, kid? A little thin on Christmas spirit with that robbery at the end."

"I guess so." I was starting to feel a little sorry for myself again.

"Hey, what's the matter? Stranded? Parents never made it?"

"No," I said.

"Well, where are they?"

Then it occurred to me—I didn't necessarily have to go back to the hotel. Maybe I shouldn't. With the Oboe Man missing, maybe I should try to find Mom first. Just in case.

"My mom's at a fort, I think." If the Oboe creep was right.

"A fort, huh? Come over here." Caen motioned for me to follow, and I went with him right past the police—he nodded and waved to one of the officers—to a little area behind their squad cars, where a small handful of people were waiting around. A few yards away from them, a man stood by some trees, puffing a cigarette.

"The VIP lounge, kiddo. The cops let the swellest of swells hang out back here. If they don't question them soon, these people will send their butlers and maids up from Atherton and down from Pacific Heights to stand in for 'em." We came up to the man near the trees. "Hey, Joe, know any good forts?"

The man stepped out from the shadows.

"Forts, huh? Well, there's Fort Funston, out on the Army base."

It was him. Joe DiMaggio! He nodded toward me.

"Nice cap, kid."

"It's the Seals."

"I know."

"Kid"—this time it was Caen talking—"meet Joe DiMaggio."

DiMaggio nodded again. "I don't like to give autographs, though. Just so you know."

I had my hand sticking out to shake his, but then put it back in my pocket.

"What does your ma do?" Caen asks.

How much should I tell them? I don't want to keep lying about a situation I haven't figured out yet myself.

"She's . . . she's a scientist," I said.

"She working on the war effort?" Caen asked.

"I think so."

DiMaggio shrugged. "Maybe she's out at Fort Point."

"Where's that?" I thought maybe I could walk.

"Right under the Golden Gate Bridge, kid, but it's sealed off. A lot of crazy rumors about top-secret war stuff going on there. I think you'll just have to wait for your mom to get home."

"I'd like to try and get in anyway."

"Well, kid, you'll still need to take a cab. Here." Caen handed me a five-dollar bill. "Buy yourself a milk shake later on, too. I'd tell Joe to take ya, but he never brings his car anywhere." DiMaggio gave us a kind of panicked look as Caen continued. "Sorry I can't stay. Gotta talk to a couple folks here and buzz down to the paper to write this up before the *Call Bulletin* scoops us. Merry Christmas, kid!"

He tipped his hat and was gone. DiMaggio stood there, smoking, and nodded at me but didn't say anything else. I realized I was getting pretty hungry. I'd only eaten a couple of those crepe things. So I asked him about his restaurant. I read once that he had one.

"You own a spaghetti place, right?"

His look wasn't panic this time, but more like puzzlement, like why the heck was I bothering him about noodles at a time like this. "A fish place. Joe DiMaggio's Grotto. Down in North Beach. But you can get a good plate of pasta there."

"Do you eat there all the time?"

"It's too crowded for me. To tell you the truth, kid, in the off-season, I try to avoid crowds."

He goes silent again, and it's kind of weird that I have to keep the conversation going, since I'm the one they all keep calling "kid."

"Well, you had a really great year, right?" I ask. In the '41 season, he had a record hitting streak.

"Yeah, they're celebrating it over at the Grotto," he answers. "Put on a party for me. I hit in fifty-six consecutive games this past season. Helluva thing. It's a record."

"Yeah, and it's never—" I catch myself. I've really got to watch it. "I bet it'll never be broken. You must be proud of yourself."

"Yeah, sure, but like I said, it's almost like someone else did it. I can't just play baseball anymore. I can't just *play.* I have to be *him.* It's just not fun anymore."

Wow, if playing baseball for a living isn't fun, grownups must have really depressing lives. "I should tell you about Barnstormers."

"What's that?"

"A game. Like—" I don't want to mess up another detail here and seem any more *po*-like than I have to. Let's see, before games were electronic they were mostly—"a *board* game. Where you manage your own baseball team. The whole squad is made up of these really messed-up monsters who go around from town to town, playing exhibition games, pickup games, whatever they can. Because they *love* it. Of course, after each game, they get chased away and have to go somewhere else."

"Messed-up monsters? Sounds like some Red Sox fans I've seen."

"On my team, Wolfman plays your position. Center field."

Even in the dark, I can see DiMaggio looking at me a moment. "Center field, huh? Does he have a hitting streak?"

"He's not bad."

He reaches into a pocket and hands me a piece of paper. It's some kind of flyer or pamphlet.

"What's this?"

"Read it. I figure a guy who manages werewolves might be able to make sense of it."

DO YOU KNOW WHERE
THE HOLY GRAIL IS?
THE GERMAN HIGH COMMAND DOES!
THE NAZIS ARE COLLECTING
— POWERFUL OBJECTS —

Such as the Spear of Destiny,
the Holy Grail, and Excalibur—
King Arthur's Dragon Sword!

"The Dragon Sword," I tell him, tapping my finger on the word *Excalibur.* "They had a fake one inside the museum."

"Keep reading, kid. It gets worse."

The possessor of these objects could wield
GREAT POWER!!

No government should be allowed to own them!

No government should be asleep!

Demand an investigation!

Demand ACTION!!

"Corny stuff, huh?" DiMaggio's shifting around from foot to foot, like he's getting colder. Or maybe having a conversation just makes him nervous.

"What does it mean?"

"Well, if you don't know, kid, ask him." He jerks his head in the direction of a man standing by the steps of the museum, holding a sign with big letters saying WAKE UP! You could see him trying to give handouts to people who were standing outside, but nearly everyone was pretending to ignore him.

"Who knows?" DiMaggio says. "That guy

marches around my restaurant, trying to get people to take his flyers."

"Why?"

"Hollywood people go there. Sports people. He wants to get noticed. That's why he came to the museum. Figured this is where the action was tonight." He shook his head as if the sign man had done something wrong. "Everyone wants to get noticed."

"You got noticed, Mr. DiMaggio," I point out to him.

"And you know what, kid? All I wanted was to play ball well enough so I could avoid putting in all those hours on my old man's fishing boat. Here's what they used to say to me when I was starting out. . . ."

And then, to my surprise, he grabs the hat off my head. He turns it around in his hands. "Why is it all sticky like this?"

Of course I can't tell about the Thickskin, the synthetic coating that prevents direct contact with the cap, which has become some kind of supercharged, backward-traveling time particle. When I touch the cap, I get tangled up in time, heading off somewhere usually *not* of my own choosing.

"It's to protect it," I tell him. "It's valuable."

"We just sweat in 'em. Here." He takes a pen out of his coat, looks under the cap, and rubs away some of the Thickskin with his fingers. He writes on the band. Two initials: a *D* and a *B*.

"That stands for 'DiMaggio, *buon.*' That's how the old-timers wish me good luck." He hands the cap back to me, then walks over to where the squad cars are parked and taps one of the policemen on the shoulder.

"In a minute, mister, I'm still with—oh, it's you, Mr. DiMaggio."

"I really have to go now."

"Uh, did we get your statement?"

"I've been trying to tell you guys. I didn't see anything. I got here late."

The cop makes a note. "Well, okay. We just want to make sure they weren't targeting any of the celebrities."

DiMaggio makes a show of patting himself down. "I'm not missing a thing. But hey"—he nods toward me—"make sure that kid gets a ride wherever he wants to go."

"He lost?"

DiMaggio looks at me, then back at the cop. "I don't think so. Just misplaced."

Boy, I'll say!

"Okay, Mr. DiMaggio," the cop says. "Happy holidays."

"You, too." DiMaggio looks at me. "And you, too, kid."

I tap my Seals cap. "Thanks for the autograph."

He starts walking away, then pauses in the shadows. "Thanks for not asking for it."

I look at my cap a moment. Then I take a little wad of Thickskin from my pocket—I'm running low, I have to be careful—and smear it over the signed letters. I can't let any part of the cap come into contact with my skin—not until I'm ready to go.

D.B.

Danger Boy.

"DiMaggio! Joe DiMaggio!"

Someone's shouting, and I turn. It's Sign Man, who's being held by the cop DiMaggio had just talked to. Apparently he just realized Joe was here and is trying to follow him.

"Look, back off, mister."

But Sign Man ignores the cop and continues to yell after DiMaggio, even though he's disappeared from view. "Time is short! We're in bigger trouble than we know! Wake up!"

"Knock it off, buddy. I mean it."

"See for yourself!" He holds out one of the flyers, but the cop won't take it.

And then I recognize him: The bristly haircut on top of two intense eyes behind a pair of wire-rim glasses.

Andrew Jackson Williams. Who I met—meet—one night in Vinita, Oklahoma, when my dad and I were—are—driving cross-country.

To this day, I don't know what year that night took place in.

Chapter Ten

Thea: Flight and Fire

2019 C.E.

"Thea! A good time to meet!" K'lion was so excited after I crashed into his prison that he gave me what I believe to be the Saurian equivalent of a kiss—a tongue dragged up the nose toward the eyes. It leaves you a bit damp.

I told him I'd been sent to rescue him. "And you did!" he replied. "Passing grade! *Skt!* But how did you find me?"

"The ship . . . the *vessel* found you, K'lion. This is a prototype, a test model."

"Oh, very dangerous. *Snk!* Could be a sneak test. Or might just not work."

"I volunteered to pilot it. I wanted to return to Earth, to this time, to find you and Eli."

"Was this your science project?"

"It is science, but even its inventors, such as Gennt, aren't sure whose anymore: They've made the ship mostly plasmechanical now, like the lingo-spots. It *feels.* It *reacts.* It belongs, more and more, to *itself.* When I was in the Fifth Dimension, the vessel began anticipating my piloting moves, as if it were coming to . . . to *understand* me. At one point, space was stretched out so far around me and I seemed to be moving so slowly, that I fell asleep briefly. When I awoke, the ship was *humming.*"

"Humming?"

"Making music."

"A rousing Cacklaw grind march?"

"No, a lullaby my mother used to sing to me. I'd been dreaming of it. But how did the ship know?"

"Not sure either," he replied. "Stranded here myself *bt! bt!* being an outlaw and a stenonychosaurus. I'm badly behind with science and engineering journals. How does the new *kp! kp!* compass work?"

"It's no longer based only on known coordinates. After what happened to you, they realized that sticking only to the known was too limiting. It allowed them no room for surprises."

"They're courting surprise? *Kww!* What an eruption! Normally, our teachers wish to save us from true surprises until the upper-grade curriculum. And even then *snkt!* it's all kept within limits."

"Well," I told K'lion, "when you get back home, you may find that I have disrupted several syllabi and course descriptions. As for the compass . . . Gennt showed me how it works. Though I wonder if he was completely sure himself. You begin by agitating the plasma, get it to focus on the object or location being sought."

"But how?"

"Atomic structure, I believe, K'lion. The ship *knew* to seek you out. You put in . . . tissue from the person or place you seek."

"The vibrations!"

"What?"

"Vibrations!" K'lion repeated. *"Pwwt!"* He was excited. "Gennt always had a theory about vibrations humming through the universe—that each being, each planet had a different . . . *t-t-tnh! hum.* So if you had a sample of someone's atomic structure, you would have a sample of their personal . . . music."

"The ship finds people by listening to their music?"

"Can't say. I'm not the pilot. But it seems to have adapted *p-chw!* to you. *Tk-tk-tk!* What did you use for my atomic structure, since most of my atoms were here with me?"

"A bit of the eggshell that hatched you." And here he seemed to grow nostalgic.

"Ah, yes. They always save our shells. Do you have anything *klng!* of Eli's?"

It was that question that led us to Eli's

father. We thought the laboratory would be a logical place to start the search for our missing friend. Until K'lion modified his position.

"Sandusky-sire won't be there," he said. "They keep driving him out of his nest."

"Then how will we find Eli if we can't find his father?"

"We can find the sire," K'lion said. "He's not lost *kww!* in time. Just in sorrow. Pop us into Dimension Five, Thea. We should skip-jump through and arrive at night."

"Arrive where?"

"I hazard guesses." And he set the controls for some terrestrial coordinates.

We disappeared briefly into the Fifth Dimension—so quickly that there was no napping or ship music. When we reappeared, the moon was out.

We were above a low range of mountains. It was cold, but there was a campfire burning. Eli's father, Sandusky, sat next to it.

He looked up at us and smiled a little. "You got out, K'lion. That's good. And you, Thea."

He stood up and took my hands in his. "You're back."

"I don't know if I am back," I told him. "I might just be visiting." Then I realized he had no lingo-spot and couldn't understand me. K'lion would have to speak for us both.

"How'd you find me?" Sandusky asked.

"Factored in the heart," K'lion said. "Knew about the satelli-T-T-T-e overhead. Knew you'd want to stay away from the lab awhile, even Wolf House, if they could monitor you. But knew too you would not want to forget. Charted perimeter of the satellite's surveillance grid. And decided you would be just outside it, unseen but seeing." K'lion pointed down the ridge, and there below, in the distance, in the Valley of the Moon, was a glimpse of the Wolf House ruins.

Sandusky sipped something from a round, metallic cup. "Eli's gone, K'lion."

"I know."

"Back in time someplace, like his mother.

He thought he could find her and bring her back home. It's been almost a month, and there's no sign."

"Me and Thea wish to fetch-get him."

"How?"

"Tell us when he is."

Eli's father smiled at this. Momentarily. "I have reason to believe Eli's mother might be in the city of San Francisco, during a period of one of our worst Earth wars. Eli tried to go back to find her. I hope . . . he's someplace safe."

Then he looked at me. I believe he knew I could understand him. "The slow pox is getting worse here. They're talking about quarantines soon. . . . I hope we haven't done something terrible by breaking apart time like this. Not just 'we' as in all people. But 'we' as in my family, specifically. As in *me.* Specifically." He sipped again from his cup. "It doesn't feel like anything . . . can be *controlled* anymore."

Slow pox. The epidemic that was raging in

my city of Alexandria when Eli and K'lion first appeared out of time. Apparently the authorities here wanted Eli to deliberately bring a sample of the disease back, so they could study it. Mother always said the only reliable part of an experiment was its unpredictable side. The virus escaped.

It appears the very act of creating virus cultures from the scrolls and animal skins they brought forward in time created the same epidemic that compelled them to go look for the virus in the first place. Like a big circle, or the giant mirrors in Pharos's lighthouse back home, endlessly reflecting each other. But I wanted to tell Sandusky his time experiments brought good results, too. If Eli had not come back in time, they would have surely taken my life when they took Mother's. I have no home, but I am alive.

"Our ship needs direction," K'lion said. "Specific to *f-chng!* finding Eli."

"Well, in Earth terms, I think the year would

be 1940 or 1941. Or maybe, by now, '42. I can't be quite sure."

"More, please," K'lion requested.

"You mean a season? A month?" Eli's father asked.

"An object. This is a new vessel, with new gears. Thea *t-t-t-ttt!* knows it. Vessel itself sniffs out beings in spacetime. Just needs a little atomic structure from the thing being sought."

Eli's father nodded. "WOMPER radiation."

"What is WOMPER?" K'lion asked.

"Wide Orbital Massless Particle Reverser," Sandusky said. "Your scientists probably have a different name. Fundamental particles of the universe that determine the 'time change' of everything. Forward or backward. We're just—*I'm* just—now learning how to track them, to use them. Everything—every being, emits a slightly different . . . WOMPER halo, we could call it. Because everything—living or not—is just a little somewhere different in spacetime than everything else. Like a cosmic fingerprint.

No two are alike." He shrugged and sat down by the fire. "All these splendid theories, yet our families have been torn apart."

"Particles come together in strange *hkk-kk-khh!* ways. Me and Thea now with you. Three beings, three different times, two separate species, two parallel planets. Who knows how many dimensions between us before? Odd combinations, yet here we are. Let us search *kt!* for Eli."

Sandusky sipped from his cup again and looked at both of us. "Well, if you're really going after him. . . ." He reached in carefully to the pocket of his garment and drew out a small piece of parchment. "I found an old paper of his when I was cleaning up. I've been carrying it around."

He handed it to K'lion, and we both looked at it in the firelight. I couldn't read the markings of their language, but K'lion could. "Barnstormer Robot Man!" he said aloud. Below it was a child's drawing of a mechanical man.

"He's loved that game for as long as I can

remember. His fingerprints are all over the paper. But they're old. He was little." Sandusky paused, and his eyes wandered over to the fire. "I don't know if that'll help you get a WOMPER reading on him or not. But bring it back. Bring someone back. Bring something."

K'lion said we would. I'm not versed much in their modern tongue, but I did learn "bye." So that's what I said. And I kissed him on the cheek.

Sandusky of the Sands nodded, and we went back into the ship, which had begun to hum again.

I showed K'lion again what Gennt had shown me: the scanning panel that allows new material to be absorbed by the plasmechanical direction finder. It worked to take me to K'lion. Now we would see if it worked to take us to Eli.

Chapter Eleven

Eli: Sign Man

December 24, 1941 C.E.

"I know you," I say to Andrew Jackson Williams.

He doesn't seem one hundred percent surprised. "Where are you from?" he asks.

"Here and there," I tell him.

"I moved to California from Vinita, Oklahoma. To spread the good word. But you're not from back home, are you?"

"Not that home. Not really." How do you tell someone you've met him, but *not yet*? The answer is, you don't. I've probably already said too much. "What's the good word?"

He taps his flyer. "The Nazis are collecting power objects." He motions over his shoulder. "And now one has been taken from that museum. I wanted to keep a close watch, but it's already too late. And the exhibit hasn't opened yet. I believe they were after the sword."

"No, I saw it. It was a fake."

"You were in there?" He seems genuinely surprised.

"Yeah. But they weren't after the sword. They took antlers."

"The White Stag's antlers!"

"How do you know about all this stuff?" I ask. Does he already know that in his future, he gets caught in a rip in spacetime, and that Thirty and Mr. Howe and a bunch of people from DARPA will be showing me his picture on the news? "Have you ever heard of DARPA?"

"DARPA," he whispers. Then he pulls me away from the police cars. "Is that the name of the project?"

Just then, a few cabs roll up. Either the cops have all their statements or people don't care and are going to leave anyway. One of the taxis pulls up near us, and a young couple, both in fancy clothes, rushes over to it. Before the man gets in the car, he scowls at us, then stuffs a dollar into my hand. Then he turns to Andrew Jackson Williams. "Shame on you, bringing your kid out here to beg with you on Christmas Eve!"

With that, he slams the door. They're probably headed to DiMaggio's Grotto, toward a nice big plate of hot spaghetti with warm garlic toast. They should get some chocolate rice milk to go with it, but I bet they won't.

Has rice milk been invented yet?

"Seen any *po* tonight?" says a voice from another cab.

"Charlie!"

"I heard on the radio there was some trouble here. I came back to see if you were all right." He motions to the people waving down the other taxis. "Didn't realize it'd be so good for business. You need another ride, kid?" Then he looks at Andrew Jackson. "Oh, did your dad come back?"

"I'm not the boy's father," Andrew Jackson corrects him, before I can. "But I can tell the child has aptitude."

"He's not my dad, Charlie. And Margarite isn't my teacher. She's my mom. And I'm still looking for her."

Charlie looks like he has a bunch more questions for me, but I guess he hears a lot of stories, so he decides to leave mine alone for now.

"Well, hop in. You won't even have to pay me any spooky money," he says with a grin. "Where is she?"

"She might be back at the hotel by now."

"Has your mother gone missing?" Andrew Jackson asks. He seems suspicious. Not of me—but of the simple fact she's gone.

"Not exactly," I tell him. "Hey, I can just call you A.J., right?"

He cocks an eyebrow. "Not just aptitude, but perhaps the gift. How do you know that?"

"You told—" I stop. "You look like that could be your nickname."

"Strange things are afoot tonight. But then, Christmas Eve is a night of heightened expectation."

"Look, before we go," I tell them, "I should find a phone and see if my mom returned to the Fairmont."

There's a slight pause as they wait for me to go off and make my call. "Um, I might need somebody to show me how to do it." I guess I can use the five-dollar bill that Caen gave me, if I can figure out how to slide it in. They don't have anything simple like vidphones or wallet cards.

"You really are from out of town," Charlie says.

"You don't know the half of it."

"We can just use my radio. I'll ask one of the cabbies there to check with the front desk. Get in." Charlie flings open the door for me, and I climb inside. "What's your mom's full name again, kid? Something like French?"

"Margarite Sands," I tell him. "But she might be going by Franchon."

A.J. has been standing outside the car, fidgeting with his sign. I think he was waiting to be invited inside. But when he hears me, he starts pulling some other crumpled paper from his pockets.

"She's not there," Charlie tells me, putting his radio microphone back. "Any other ideas?"

"Well, there's this fort. . . ."

"Fort Point," A.J. croaks. His eyes are on fire again behind those glasses. "Fort Point," he repeats.

"Why do you say that?"

He slides into the cab and holds up a paper so Charlie and I can see it. It's just a printed list of names. But it says *Samuel Gravlox Orchestra—Undercover* on the top.

A few of the names are circled. Including, halfway down, the name of Margarite Franchon. My mom.

"How did you get this?" I ask.

"I think she could be in great danger. Is she at the fort tonight?"

"She wouldn't tell me where she was going."

A.J. turns to Charlie. "Can you get us to Fort Point?"

Charlie shakes his head. "It's behind the base. Whole area's been restricted for months."

A.J. nods. "Actually, I misspoke. Can you get us to the Golden Gate Bridge?"

"Sure. But why?"

"There's a way down to the fort. It's dangerous, but I think we need to risk it. We need to warn the people there. We need to warn this boy's mother."

"Warn her of what?"

Before he can answer, the cop that Joe DiMaggio was talking to walks up and leans in the window. A.J. is so startled it looks like he might shoot off the seat and hit the cab's roof.

"Hey, kid." The cop gives both Charlie and A.J. the once-over. "You okay? DiMaggio wanted me to look after you."

"I'm fine, officer. In fact we're going to . . . DiMaggio's Grotto! To get some pasta." It's my stomach talking, but it sounds reasonable enough.

"Well, all right, kid. If you're sure." He looks at A.J., then back at me. "He going with you?"

"Yup. Family friend. Merry Christmas!" I wave as Charlie puts the cab in gear and pulls away before the officer can think of any more questions.

We drive through the park and come out in one of the neighborhoods, with its square blocks and pressed-together houses. But the streets are empty, and for a moment it feels like we could be the only three people in the world.

I turn back to A.J. and repeat my earlier question. "Warn my mom about what?"

He's leaning back against the seat, his eyes closed, as if what he knows is already pressing down on him. "She and everyone else on her secret project are about to be betrayed."

It feels like one of the longest cab rides of

my life. Of course, it's only about the second cab ride of my life.

Charlie knows something serious is happening, but he's trying to make small talk, mostly for my benefit, I think, since he's figured out my mom's in danger.

"I really like all that crazy stuff you were saying about them Barnies," he says.

"Barnstormers," I tell him.

"I mean, the whole idea of monsters playing sports. It's great! Like we coulda had the *po* out there on Maui, playing the Seals! People woulda paid high money for that! But"—and here he seems to pick his words a little more carefully—"nobody's really making a game like that, are they?"

"Not yet," I admit. A.J. gives me a funny look.

"'Cause I been writin' ideas down, if you don't mind." He holds up a pad of paper. "I mean, I don't want to be drivin' a cab forever. Gotta miss my family like this on Christmas Eve and stuff!"

I want to find out more from A.J. Williams about why my mom is in danger and how he could know any of that, but he's trying to be all hush-hush, like saying anything else in front of Charlie could be dangerous.

I'm getting more worried, getting that knot-in-my-stomach feeling, so to take my mind off it, I follow Charlie's lead and talk about Barnstormers, and I really start to wonder whether he could invent the game before the company that's supposed to does.

I know that Barnstormers really *was* a kind of board game at first—way, way back, before my parents were born and before there was a Comnet. And the company that makes it is . . .

Dang Good Games.

Dang!

If I had enough room right now, I'd fall out of my seat.

"You could be the future!" I blurt out. A.J. almost bounces off his seat again.

"Who could be the future, son?"

I'm excited, but I still don't want to alarm anybody. "Any of us. Any of us could be."

"Any of us *could* be the future. But none of us knows what that future is." A.J. gives me another of his looks. "But some people are trying to find out."

"*Who?*" I wish he'd just come out and say what he knows. But maybe he doesn't want to alarm *me.* Still, we're talking about finding my mom. "What do you mean? Look, you better tell me how you got that piece of paper with my mother's name on it—"

The cab screeches to a halt.

I don't know exactly where we are, but looking through the cab window, I can see the towers of the Golden Gate Bridge in the distance. But there's a roadblock, like a storm has come through: a fallen tree lies across the pavement, along with several boulders. We're not going to be driving over that bridge anytime soon.

A.J. is the first one to open a door and step outside.

"What's happening?" I ask.

"Part one: They got the antlers. Part two: They don't want anyone else to get 'em."

"What do you mean?"

"I mean, this isn't an accident. Everyone's makin' their moves tonight. If you want to get to your mama, we better start walkin'."

"I need you to tell me what you know."

"I will," he said. "While we move out."

I feel a little better to see that Charlie is right behind us. His coat is pulled tight around him, and he's shaking his head and muttering about all the crazy *po*.

Chapter Twelve

Thea: Peenemünde

Early 1940s C.E.

The ship didn't take us to Eli. At least, I hope he was never there.

I'm trying to record the experience now, as we head back through the Fifth Dimension in search of our friend, but I never know how long the journey will take.

After parting from Eli's father, we returned to the void, and coming out, landed with a thud.

The ship's door opened, and blisteringly cold winds rushed in. After a little hesitation, K'lion and I stepped into a land of ice.

There was no city there. There was nothing.

We were at the top of the world, it seemed, a place we could only speculate about back in Alexandria.

But it was real enough.

I gathered my *sklaan* around me. It helped warm me a little, though my teeth chattered. K'lion seemed only slightly better protected against the elements. His hide was turning a deep gray.

The chill made it all the more startling when we saw a group of six approaching us on the ice, all of them in rags and nearly barefoot.

Somehow they didn't seem especially surprised that a girl and lizard man should be stepping out of a flying time-craft. But then, they didn't look prone to surprise: They were caked with dirt, emaciated. They looked like slow pox victims laid hurriedly to rest in Alexandrian catacombs, then somehow brought back, if only partially, to life.

One of them spoke to me. I believed it to be a woman, but intending them no disrespect, they were all so worn down it was hard to tell.

"So it's true? The Nazis have been to the moon and back? Is that where you're from?" The others remained silent. "Have you come to kill us?"

I did not answer. I was still too stunned by the whole situation. Who were they? How did they get there?

And why were we brought there?

That haunted group of people may have had the same questions for us. They looked at K'lion, motioning to each other, slowly pointing. When they whispered, the lingo-spot couldn't pick up their language clearly, although I recognized it as Teutonic in origin—some northern tribal dialect. The woman who appeared to be their leader spoke up again, pointing at my lizard friend.

"Is he a genetic experiment?"

"Must be," one of the others said. "Yet he's smiling."

There was silence between us, filled by the cold. "Well," the leader finally decided, "if you're not going to kill us, we'll keep going over the ice."

They turned away. "You'll freeze," I said to them.

They stopped, but they didn't understand me. "What language is that?" I heard one of them ask.

Without hesitating, I took a little of the lingo-spot from my skin. I could spare only enough for the leader, but if she understood me, she could tell others. I reached for her—and she looked terrified. I touched her behind the ear. I don't know what she thought I was going to do, but she shook, then dropped to her knees and started sobbing.

"Don't cry," I told her. "What's wrong?"

Startled, she looked up at me, wide-eyed. "I understand you," she whispered. Then, croaking, as if she wasn't used to talking loudly, she said to the others, "This one's an angel. Our misery is over. We're not on Earth anymore."

I hoped that we still were. "I'm not an angel. My name is Thea. What's yours?"

"Hannah," she said simply, then looked

away, as if she'd decided she couldn't have direct eye contact with me.

I liked her name. It reminded me—a little—of "Hypatia," my mother's name.

"Where are we, Hannah?"

"If we are still on Earth, then we're in its coldest hell."

"Where?"

"Peenemünde." She pointed through the fog, through the mist coming up off the ice. I could barely make out low mountains. "There. In the distance. The Germans' rocket base. Right now, you're in the middle of the Baltic Sea. But it's December. It freezes."

"And what are you doing out here, Hannah?"

"Escaping. Or dying as we try."

"Escaping what?"

She turned to look at me again, not in amazement, but something else. A touch of scorn?

"You must know. You're an angel. You've been to the moon." She tilted her head back slightly, in the direction of the mountains, but declined to look there. In the wisps of fog and cold I now saw smoke. A handful of modern chariot-like vehicles, the horseless ones, were heading toward us.

"Let them come," Hannah hissed.

"Are they the ones who did this to you?" I asked.

She nodded.

"On purpose?" K'lion asked.

"They're Nazis," she replied. I didn't know what a Nazi was, but already I dreaded meeting one.

Behind me, the ship—the ship itself—began a low humming, as it did during the search for K'lion. Hannah's eyes widened a little bit.

I took the *sklaan* from around my shoulders and wrapped it around her. "Go," I told her. "Go. This will keep you warm."

"But the Nazis—"

"We will stop them."

"How?"

"Just go." Hannah touched the *sklaan*—

"Like angel wings," she murmured—then took it off *her* shoulders and wrapped it around a little girl.

"Thank you," Hannah said. "Make sure you find out about the Hammer Cave. Please." The request was in her eyes, too. Then she turned back to her group, and they shuffled off across the ice.

For the first time since I had the honor of knowing him, I could not detect a smile on K'lion's face.

Moments later, the Nazi vehicles arrived.

The ship kept humming.

Uniformed men disembarked from the vehicle. But the particular uniform scarcely mattered—soldiers are almost always the same. They reminded me of Romans.

They unsheathed their weapons. In my short time in Earth's future, I had learned quickly about guns.

The small regiment surrounded the ship. They looked at K'lion and me, and seemed a little less sure of themselves. "A flying disk," one of them said. "So it's true."

"Is this von Braun's?" another one asked. They didn't know I could understand them.

"There are so many secrets here. Even from us," the first one replied. Then he pointed to Hannah in the distance, reaching for his weapon.

"No!" I commanded. "No!"

It wasn't in their language, but the meaning was clear. They stopped. "What if they really are from under the Earth?" the first one continued. "The Over-Beings the Fuehrer always talks about. Especially the dragon man. Didn't Hitler say creatures like that appear to him in visions?"

"Hitler says a great many things." From the others' reactions, it appeared the soldier who said that had just put himself at risk.

"What about the escapees?"

"This is more important right now."

It occurred to me the best thing would be to

get back on the ship and leave. That thought was interrupted by the *click* of their guns.

We were prisoners now, too. Hence we'd need to create the illusion of as much strength as possible.

"Von Braun," I said to them. "Von Braun." It sounded like he might be the one who oversaw the operation here. "The Hammer Cave," I added. I said it the way Hannah did, in her native tongue.

The soldiers looked at one another, then motioned for us to get into their chariots, their land-ships.

"A truck," K'lion said, in their language. A couple of them visibly jumped.

They gave him his own seat in the rear, and kept their rifles pointed at him all the way back to Peenemünde.

Chapter Thirteen

Thea: Hammer Cave

Early 1940s C.E.

We were escorted back across the ice to the island of Peenemünde, to the place Hannah and her companions were trying to escape—the Hammer Cave. It was actually a whole complex of caves linked together by tunnels.

Most of the occupants appeared to be slaves, and I could see why they'd risk their lives to leave: It was like Hades—mostly dark, and either chillingly cold or savagely hot, depending how close you were to the massive furnaces that burned in the center of the complex.

There was a large network of metal roadways—"railways," K'lion called them—leading toward the interior, where it appeared the main labor was to build "rockets," long, tapered vessels intended for . . . exploration? Destruction?

Perhaps both.

As the self-propelled chariot, the "truck," drove deeper into the cave, men, women, children, all in the barest rags, mostly skin and bones, listlessly stepped out of our way. Except for one older man, who couldn't move fast enough. The truck knocked him down and drove over his leg.

We could hear the crunch of snapping bones as we left him behind.

Our captors—our "hosts"—didn't even slow down.

But neither could any of the worker-slaves afford to stop and help him. Their faces were hollow and haunted; they may have been too worn-down to offer aid. Or to risk it. They all had numbers tattooed onto their arms, and I imagine they were carefully tracked.

Numbers. In this future, then, even having a name was an act of defiance.

Some of the slaves, the prisoners (or even, worst of all, the "guests," as I heard one soldier joke about them), were forced to push or pull wagons along the railways, hauling heavy parts for the further construction of the rockets. Others worked on the tunnels themselves, digging farther into the earth to make this complex larger and, presumably, more useful for its masters.

But to what ultimate end?

When slaves grew fatigued, they were beaten or otherwise punished. We saw one young man get hit savagely in the stomach by one of the guards when he couldn't keep lifting. He crumpled over, tried to throw up, then lay still.

For sustenance, they seemed to be given crusts of bread and thin soup. Twice I witnessed family members forcibly separated, in what appeared to be the processing of new captives.

On several occasions, K'lion was about to jump from the truck and help these poor souls, but I tugged his tail to communicate that he shouldn't move. I knew they would harm my friend as well.

"Somebody *tktt!* has to rectify the bullying," he whispered to me.

"I know." The truck stopped, and our hosts gestured with their weapons that we were to walk the rest of the way.

Some of the slaves stared at K'lion as we passed, but most did not. Even their sense of wonder had been stripped from them.

We were eventually led toward quarters that seemed to be the working precincts of the military commanders. They certainly weren't comfortable enough for actual living.

I overheard the soldiers who brought us in saying to the others that we were to wait for "von Braun."

"Von Braun will know what to do with them."

"Perhaps. If von Braun even knows what or who they are. Maybe they crash-landed. Maybe we weren't supposed to find them at all. I told you this mountain's full of secrets. Even for us."

One of their leaders walked in, a man introducing himself as a "kernel." I didn't know what that ranking meant, but his military bearing reminded me of a Roman *praefectus*—the man who leads the horse troops.

The other men all deferred to him, even seemed a little frightened. When he walked over to me, I met his gaze.

"Just some spoiled little girl," he said loudly, for the others. "Not even Aryan." Then he turned away, dismissing me with his hand. "Why was she brought here? What's this I hear about spacemen?"

They tried to tell him about the ship. They pointed to K'lion, who now had guards clustered around him. The *praefectus* examined him for a long moment. "A very interesting freak," he said. "We shall have to cut him up and examine him." I think he chose those words as a kind of test—he was watching K'lion's eyes.

"That *k-t-kh!* would be rudeness extreme!" K'lion replied. But he said it in my language, not theirs. I had never seen him choose not to respond to an Earthling in his native tongue before. It meant he'd lost trust in them completely.

"He speaks," the *praefectus* said. "He almost sounds human. So these two came from a flying disk, parked somewhere on the ice?" he asked the soldiers skeptically. They told him someone had gone to make recordings and images of our vessel, but they swore, yes, it was true.

"Well, keep your guns on them. We'll let von Braun look them over, if the great Wernher ever deigns to get here."

"He deigns, Colonel Middlekant, he deigns." Heads turned, and there was the man I assumed to be von Braun, in a white tunic-like garment, covering what I took to be civilian clothes from the era. It certainly wasn't a military uniform like the *praefectus* wore.

"What is this claptrap about a spaceship?" von Braun bellowed. The men pointed to me and then K'lion. He walked over, looked at me carefully, ran a finger over my forehead. And nodded.

Then, like the *praefectus,* he walked over to K'lion but still didn't say anything. Instead, he took out a pencil and poked K'lion in the face.

"*Yaagh!*" K'lion exclaimed.

"Interesting," von Braun replied, scribbling something down on a small tablet. "We shall have to keep him for observation. Perhaps the Allies are running genetic experiments, too. In the future, you know, everyone will."

"But—" one of the foot soldiers began. The *praefectus* and von Braun stared at him. He suddenly seemed terrified at having spoken out.

"Finish," the *praefectus* commanded.

"But what if the lizard man *is* from the center

of the Earth? What if he's an Ancient One? Didn't our Fuehrer tell us there are beings—"

And here von Braun slapped him across the face.

"We build rockets to carry explosives to foreign cities and German soldiers to the moon. No matter what the Fuehrer says, I will not waste my energy on trying to contact space aliens, find the Holy Grail, or discover the secrets of time travel! This is all nonsense! The Reich should stand for empirical science!"

Mother believed in science, too. But not as an excuse to hurt people.

"Who is this girl? This little brown-skinned girl?" Von Braun squeezed my chin, forcing me to look at him. "Why did you come, hmm? How did you get all these men to believe you have a ship? Did the Americans send you? Why are you here?"

He was really hurting me.

Why were we there? I didn't know.

I prayed it wasn't to find Eli. Not in that place. It horrified me. But I was to see worse.

Chapter Fourteen

Eli: Drachenjungen

December 24, 1941 C.E.

I can't believe what I've just been through in the last hour. My life is in danger—I nearly drowned a few seconds ago—but it's the picture of the mother and child I can't shake.

I only glimpsed them a little while ago in a wrinkled photograph that A.J. had, and I only saw *that* for a moment in the wind, under the flickering glow of a lighter held by Charlie.

"Right here's where I baptized Dan, and right over there's where he confessed." Facts and figures have been spilling out of A.J. ever since we left the car. He spoke in between huffs and puffs and grunts, as we tried to stay out of the way of patrol cars heading out to investigate the wreckage on the road, and scrambled down the cliffs to the beach.

If I thought I was cold before, I was even colder now, by the ocean at night.

Apparently A.J. knows all these back routes because he used to work here, on this army base, the Presidio—but not as a preacher, as a cook.

"Preachin's what I did on the side," he explained. "Makin' scrambled eggs and potatoes and chipped beef with gravy was what I did in the main. But the preachin's what got me known. I would just come down to the beach and start talkin' about visions I had, about how the world was gonna be changed forever in our time, and not necessarily in good ways. About how those who knew what was happening had to stick together."

It was funny, but in a way A.J. sounded like Mr. Howe. Howe is always saying there's only a handful of people who really know what's going on. But he would never use a phrase like "stick together." Howe's the kind of guy who says you have to use secrets to fight secrets.

But whatever it was that A.J. was saying, apparently he'd get people down here on the beach to listen "crack of dawn on Sunday mornings." And as he talked more about these visions he was having, he'd eventually get people coming up afterward or drawing him aside and telling him things.

"Unburdening themselves" is how A.J. described it as we stumbled through some bushes on the way toward the shore. "Because the unspoken things in this world are becoming more and more terrible."

So army guys who were getting pictures from Europe of places called "death camps," with "gas chambers" in them, would come to A.J. to tell him about what they were seeing, things they couldn't put in the newspapers here. "Things like this," A.J. said as he held the picture out. It was a fuzzy black-and-white print, showing a mother in a heavy overcoat clutching a child. She's turned away from a German soldier who points a gun at her back. He's about to kill the woman and child. Maybe with the same shot.

Even in the dark, under a sputtering lighter, the image was burned into my brain. What was that soldier thinking? He had a mother. He might even have been a father.

What kind of orders could possibly force someone to do a thing like that?

"German government got machine-gun squads in eastern Europe, goin' around, takin' Jews, Gypsies, whoever they don't like, linin' 'em up and killin' 'em all. They let the bodies fall in ditches. Then they force other people to help bury the bodies before they kill those people, too."

The lighter was blown out by the wind. "It doesn't feel much like Christmas anymore," Charlie said.

A.J. shook his head. "The common people ain't safe after this war. Both sides are trying to build rockets, and bombs that blow up entire cities all at once. They're workin' on breakin' atoms apart, too."

He meant nuclear weapons. It was weird to think about a time when they weren't around. Them or the laser and space weapons that would come later.

I mean, you just grow up assuming there's a chance the world could be blown up one day. You don't think about it; it's just there. I wonder what it was like to be a kid *before* they could blow everything up—did everyone feel safer?

"That's not all. They're workin' on time travel, too. Both sides."

"That's not possible," Charlie said, sitting down in the sand. "Now you're the one telling ghost stories."

Without thinking about it, I brushed the cap on my head. How could I tell Charlie that it *was* possible?

Except they didn't have time travel back here in 1941. Speaking from personal experience, that didn't happen until 2019.

No, wait. Mom was blasted back into time, and that was just over a year before I went. And then there's Thea, who I took across the Fifth Dimension with me, to save her from the fires and the mobs in Alexandria.

And she was born hundreds of years ago.

Maybe something *is* wrong with history now.

"Well, if they're ghosts, they're all wearin' uniforms and street clothes, and they're all holed up over there"—A.J. pointed—"trying to bend time itself."

All I could see was the tide, the bluffs above us, and the Golden Gate Bridge looming ahead. "You can't see it from here," A.J. continued. "They're in Fort Point. It's under the bridge on this side. The only way to get to it is through the water."

"We have to swim in the ocean? At night?" Charlie's looking a little more agitated than he did about the time travel.

"There's a boat tied to some pilings. We can use it to get around the bluffs, then row back in toward the fort. But we'll run into guards soon enough. Our only hope is to convince them that we know everyone working on Project Split Second is in danger."

"How do you even know what it's called?" I asked him. I was getting really annoyed that everyone seemed to know what my mom was up to but me.

"Because I baptized Dan Sterning in these waters one Sunday morning, Eli, and he confessed to me. He's been giving classified information to the Germans."

Dan the Oboe Man. "He's a spy?"

And he was trying to date my mom.

"Evidently he has family back in Europe. They're in a camp somewhere." A.J. had stepped into the tide. "We have to work our way around these boulders here. The boats are kept in a little cove on the other side. Normally, I prefer parking by the bridge and climbing down the metal girders underneath."

"You do?" No wonder this guy made such

a good preacher—he wasn't afraid to dunk people in freezing water at the crack of dawn on Sundays. "Why did Dan tell you all this?"

"We all got family, son. He feels he ain't got any choice but to protect his."

"How come you didn't tell somebody?"

"I'm not allowed to share what people confess to me. It's sacred. And secret. Between preacher and parishioner. That's why they feel free to talk. But I told Dan to tell someone else. To confess what he'd done and make amends."

He suddenly lapsed into silence.

"Well, what happened?"

"I guess he told somebody *something*. But it wasn't a confession. The captain came and discharged me from my cook's job. Said I was sufferin' from delirium, talkin' about time travel and all. Thing is, I never mentioned it to him. Must've been Dan, not quite able to own up to what was happening, probably saying I told him about Project Split Second. Captain probably doesn't even know what's going on under his own nose. They're tellin' people they're usin' Fort Point as medical quarters for sick infantrymen. Nobody knows what's really goin' on there. Not even most of the army folk."

"But you do?" Maybe coming out here with A.J. wasn't such a smart idea, after all. What if A.J. *was* delirious? "And that's why you're telling us about his confession?"

"Dan broke the covenant, son. And he used my pledge of secrecy to make matters worse. Now the Nazis are convinced that Project Split Second is on the verge of success. And they've been frustrated because they haven't been able to figure out how to travel through time on their own."

"So what are the Nazis doing about it?"

A.J. didn't answer; he walked out farther on the rocks in the water. "Careful. It's slippery. Don't fall in."

"Ow!" That was Charlie. "Something stung me!"

"Jellyfish. Be careful. We gotta be quiet. We don't want them shooting at us."

Shooting at us! How come, if I have to be

tangled up in time, I can't land in some *peaceful* moment in history?

The rocks were slick, and I almost lost my footing and went under several times.

A.J. was just ahead of us, but with only the light from a partial moon overhead, I couldn't really see him clearly—besides, my eyes were stinging from the saltwater spray churning out of the sea.

A.J. crawled around the corner of the largest rock, then disappeared. I didn't hear anything, but kept going.

"A.J.?" I said, but I could barely even hear myself in the wind.

"Andrew Jackson!" I shouted, but still nothing.

"You all right?" Charlie had come up right behind me.

"I think so," I told him, but my teeth were chattering pretty badly. "I guess he must be waiting for us by that boat."

I turned the corner on the rock—almost falling in again—and saw the small cove ahead of us. A.J. was already there, and he had some kind of light—had he made a fire?—glowing on the narrow strand of beach.

"A.J.?"

I bumped into something, figuring at first it might be the rowboat.

But it wasn't. Not unless rowboats were about twenty feet long.

"What—?" Then I heard roaring all around, and my feet went out from under me completely, and I was drifting underwater, under the cold saltwater, thinking about all the places in time I'd like to see, thinking about that picture of the mother and child A.J. showed me, and how sad it was, it is, how sad that that's what's happening in this world, in this time. . . .

My world. Soldiers just following orders, and what about me? What about me? As Danger Boy, Danger . . . Danger . . . Danger Boy, they wanted me to go on secret missions for them, for Mr. Howe, for Thirty; to follow orders, everyone just following orders, no matter what, like everything is in the past, even our futures, because we're all stuck doing what we always do, as if it's already written down somewhere, in some old-fashioned book or on some Comnet history review with pictures . . . all our pictures . . . with Barnstormer pictures . . . I used to be little when I played that game . . . that Dang Good Game . . . I used to be little . . . a little boy, but I'm growing up now . . . growing up . . . blacking up . . . blacking out . . . I'm blacking out—

And then I was slapped hard, and found myself on the beach coughing and soaking wet. In the dark I could just make out a little glint of light on the rims of A.J.'s glasses.

"You all right, son? Looks like Charlie and I pulled you out just in time."

I nod. I'm about to ask him something else when I notice we've been joined by several others—guys I don't recognize, in wool caps and heavy coats; they look like sailors. I guess they come with the giant boat.

One of them leans over to stare at my face.

He acts like he recognizes me. And then I recognize him: the kid from the museum. The big snotty one who knocked me over.

"You've been following me, Roy Rogers," he says.

Following him? "Who's . . . Roy Rogers?"

"All you American kids think you're Roy Rogers. Think you're cowboys. Well, too bad. We're dragons. And dragons eat cowboys."

I feel like I'm still underwater, drowning. I turn my head to look at A.J. for some kind of explanation.

"I guess they got here first," he says. "I guess Dan gave them everything they wanted."

"Quiet!" the snotty kid snaps. "I am a captain in the *Drachenjungen,* and you are our prisoners. Except we probably won't keep you."

That's when I notice what he has in his hands. The other guys are holding guns, pointed at A.J. and Charlie. But Museum Boy is clutching the White Stag's stolen antlers.

"We will add these to our collection," he announces.

"All this trouble for a pair of deer horns?" I ask.

"Not just horns. We have some tidying up to do."

It doesn't sound like he means pitching in to clean up trash on the beach, and the picture of the mother and child keeps swirling around in my head, like a song I can't get rid of, only this one keeps reminding me how messed up the world is. And here's this big jerk, acting like he's a superhero or something, and all he wants to do is make things worse.

"You think you're so tough." It sounds kind of lame, as soon as I say it.

"We *are* tough, Roy Rogers." We're both talking like we're stuck in a Comnet game or something, but that doesn't faze Museum Boy. "We're *Drachenjungen.* The finest young Aryan men in the world."

"'Dragon Youth,' son. That's what the name means," A.J. translates, and you can hear in his voice he's been hurt. "They're special soldiers.

Young ones." For all A.J.'s trouble, one of the goons hits him in the ribs.

I move to help him, but Museum Boy knocks me down into the wet sand.

"The finest young men in the world." He grins. "And I am their leader. Rolf Royd."

Rolf? Well, Rolfie thinks he's tough. But if we could just do something about those goons with guns, I bet we could take him.

"And after tonight, these fine young men will be famous," he continues. "Stay a little longer and see why. We're waiting for the fort to blow up."

The fort.

Mom.

"I'm sorry, Eli," A.J. says.

"For what?" I'm so worried, it sounds like I'm snapping at him.

"I think they've given Dan some kind of bomb to plant in the fort to blow up the time machine. Now is the time to pray for your mother's safety."

"Sei ruhig!" Rolf spits, and this time he personally kicks A.J. in the leg.

"Stop it! There aren't any time machines! Time machines haven't been invented yet!" I'm standing, almost shouting, and A.J., Charlie, Rolf, and his Boy Scouts are all staring at me.

"How do you know, son?" A.J. says quietly.

I never get to answer. We hear a large *KA-BOOM* from the other side of the bluffs. Everybody turns to it, but without even thinking, I dive at Rolf. He swings the antlers at me, hard, and they scratch my face.

He can really fight, and I can't, and I guess I'm about to get my butt kicked, but I'm still thinking about that soldier shooting the mother and her kid, and now maybe my own mom could be hurt, or worse, and all I wanted was to bring her *home*—

"Good Lord!" I don't even know who says it, and I don't want to look, but I glance out of the corner of my eye and see it, too.

"A flying saucer!" A.J. is pointing.

Flying over the Golden Gate Bridge is a ship. It looks like a time-vessel.

A Saurian time-vessel.

But not Clyne's. Not quite.

That was the explosion we heard—the boom of the ship entering this time and place.

An air-raid siren screams to life, and it's not a drill. All of us stand, watching the ship fly circles around one of the tips of the Golden Gate's towers.

History had changed again.

Chapter Fifteen

Thea: Thunderclap

Early 1940s C.E.

The man named von Braun was still holding my chin. Tears wanted to flow from my eyes, but I held them back, refusing to let him see.

If Eli was there somewhere, would we be led to him? If he wasn't, then how did we come to be there?

I tried to find an answer, to take my mind off the pain from von Braun's grip. Perhaps Eli's rendering of a mechanical man had something to do with bringing us to a place of destructive science? Could the ship have misinterpreted the Barnstormer Robot Man drawing? More and more, the new Saurian time-vessel seemed to be operating with an intelligence of its own, which neither I nor K'lion were privy to.

Von Braun let go of my chin. "This is all a ruse. A trick. Take the girl away. Take the serpent man to the medical doctors, and let them run their tests. I'm sure if you go out and look at that so-called ship, you will find it made of nothing more than lies and balsa wood. I've already lost one of my best young rocket scientists to the *Drachenjungen* so that he could volunteer for that suicide mission in San Francisco. This stupidity has to end somewhere. We don't have anything to fear from these people"—and then, with a glance at K'lion—"these beasts. Our science is, and will always be, superior to theirs."

The *praefectus* nodded. "My thoughts exactly, von Braun."

Things might have gone very badly for us just then if the vessel hadn't swooped into the Hammer Cave, humming so loudly it no longer gave off music but seemed to shriek.

That shriek was matched by the shouting and screaming from the soldiers inside the cave.

Von Braun and the *praefectus* went white, then ran out to see what was happening. In their rush, several bindings, parchment holders, and pictures were knocked from the table to the ground.

The images and writings were some kind of documentation about what these Nazis were doing in places other than the Hammer Cave. To people not as "lucky" as the slaves there. The images are still with me:

Bodies lined up by ditches—men, women, young, old. They lie still in holes in the ground. Piles of them.

Buildings of fire, with people naked, withered, haunted, and hurt beyond reason—prodded by soldiers to march inside.

And I saw the mother.

It was a lone image, there on the ground below me. A man, a soldier, was in a field. He's holding his gun, aiming it at the back of a woman, a mother, pressing her child to her chest. They are waiting for this soldier to ignite his gun, to follow his "order."

To murder them.

I know all about people following orders.

My mother, Hypatia, was murdered by people following orders in Alexandria. And that is who these "scientists" are in Peenemünde, with their new machines. Killers of children.

"Thea!" It was K'lion.

"Escape now please!" He motioned for me to come with him.

Numb, I picked up the picture of the woman and child—I don't know why—and slipped it inside my tunic. I staggered out after K'lion.

We found ourselves on a platform overlooking much of the cave below. But the *praefectus* was there, too, running at us, weapon raised.

K'lion hissed like a cat, and appeared ready to leap at the *praefectus,* but I knew my lizard friend couldn't possibly survive those kinds of weapons. They weren't mere blades he could jump away from.

But suddenly the *praefectus* was knocked forward and cracked his head on the ground.

A soldier had come to our aid—the one who was so panicked about us being "Ancient Ones" from the middle of the Earth.

"Leave! Get out of here!" he yelled. "Get out of here! Go! Tell the Fuerher we helped you and not to harm us! Get out! Get out now!"

And then the vessel rose, like a fish breaking water, next to the railing where we stood. It was still wailing—a loud, pervasive sound of agony like a whole chorus groaning at once. K'lion grabbed me and leaped off the railing, hurling us through the opened ship's hatch before it slammed closed.

The ship glittered briefly, like river water reflecting sunlight, then disappeared from the Hammer Cave.

I knew we'd left, because the colors of the Fifth Dimension swirled around us.

I was exhausted, drained. Why *did* the ship bring us to Peenemünde?

Was Eli there somewhere, and did we fail him?

Suddenly we were shaken by what sounded like claps of thunder, as if we were riding through a storm. I'd never had that experience crossing the Fifth Dimension before.

"Rough times ahead!" K'lion shouted.

As I looked through the ship's translucent sides, it seemed as if *we* were the thunderclaps: We were skittering across the Earth in quick random bursts, appearing and disappearing in an instant—first a land battle below, then somewhere at sea with ships fighting, then over a great city, bombed from the sky, and then . . .

The noise subsided, and we hovered above a field. Bodies lay scattered, just like in the images in the Hammer Cave. But this was real. I looked down—the floor had become translucent, too—and saw her below me:

The mother, holding her child. She kept her son's face buried against her. I saw the soldier behind them. He didn't look up. But she did.

She saw me. It was a look of such profound sadness and resignation that I expect it will always haunt me, no matter how many eons away I am.

"K'lion!"

It all happened so fast. The woman turned away to bury her face against her child's neck.

Thunderclap.

We were back in the Fifth Dimension.

No wonder there was no surprise on her face. In a world where such things can happen, a mere time-vessel is small cause for alarm.

Chapter Sixteen

Eli: Unsilent Night

December 24, 1941 C.E.

"We interrupt our evening of Christmas carols to bring you another report on the unidentified flying object sighted at the Golden Gate Bridge. Authorities confirm that the bridge is currently closed to all traffic, but they say this is due to unusual and dangerous wind conditions from the Pacific Ocean. Newspaper reporter Herb Caen has phoned us, saying he could definitely see lights in the sky and would try to get closer, noting he had an invite to a Christmas party at the Officers' Club in the nearby Presidio.

'Anyway,' to quote Mr. Caen, 'maybe it's Santa.' We will provide more details as we get them. Now, back to the Samuel Gravlox Orchestra's recording of 'Silent Night.'"

I turn back to Mom. "How can they keep this quiet? There's a Saurian time-ship flying around up there! My friend Clyne could be in it! How do you cover up a flying saucer and a dinosaur!?"

"All they have to do is keep newspaper pictures from getting out, Eli. There's just radio and newsprint here, no television and no Comnet." She shrugs. "But even when you have those things, you'd be surprised what can be covered up."

She takes another sip of her coffee and strokes my hair over my forehead. It's like I'm eight years old and I've been out in the snow too long. I'm sitting, shivering, with a big bulky green army sweater over me, trying to get warm.

It's great they want to get me all cozy, and that I finally found my mom, but I need to be outside right now, out there on the bridge, seeing if that's really Clyne in the ship and if he needs my help.

But they won't let anybody out of the fort.

After the time-ship appeared, Rolf began yelling to his pals on the beach. As soon as the searchlights came on, they ditched their plans to take off in the boat, and headed toward the bluffs instead. I think they wanted to stick around to make sure they heard the explosion they came for — their own bomb going off.

One of Rolf's goons figured they ought to do something about us, and the best idea he could come up with was to shoot us.

He pointed his gun at A.J., who started to say something about valleys and death, like a prayer, with his arms raised in the air. Suddenly, though, Charlie sprang to life, like he'd been waiting for the right moment, and kicked the guy just as his gun went off.

A.J. started hopping around, and I realized he'd been shot in the foot.

A.J. began cussing. Rolf and the other goon were already off the bluffs, scrambling through the brush.

Jumping on one leg, A.J. made his way over to the Germans' boat.

"I know how to drive one of these things," Charlie insisted. "Like the fast boats we had in Hawaii to hop between islands." We all climbed in, and Charlie took the wheel. "Where's the starter?"

"I don't know—I'm bleeding," A.J. said. "I expect this is it." He grabbed a handle and pulled it down. The engine roared to life, knocking me backward.

And that was as far as we got before the Navy patrols came roaring up on their way to the bridge.

They made us put our hands in the air. They didn't know if we were aliens or Germans or what, but they weren't taking any chances.

It took a while to convince them we weren't any of those things. They brought us right into Fort Point—an old brick fort that's been here since the Civil War—which they had just outfitted for their secret project.

That's where I found out that Dan the Oboe Man was under arrest—he couldn't go through with blowing up all his coworkers and wound up confessing to the Army guys. He described the German agent he'd been told to meet up with at the museum. Since he was supposed to be young, they thought at first it might be me. So they took me in to where Dan was. He was already sobbing, and as soon as he saw me, he sobbed a little harder, which didn't exactly put me in the clear right away.

But the main thing was, my mom was there, too. She was in the room with Samuel Gravlox. I guess they were telling them both about the threat to Project Split Second. Apparently, part of Dan's plan was to kidnap Mom at the de Young and use her to get into this place.

"This young man is not who you're looking for, Sergeant," she said, coming up and putting her arm around me.

"Well, then who is he?" The sergeant had

been questioning me earlier, and sounded constantly annoyed. Aides kept interrupting him with messages. They must have been about the vessel, since he kept yelling about not being able to be both *on* the bridge and *below* it at the same time.

"He's . . . a boy I know from school. At the hotel." She still didn't want to let anyone know I was her son. She didn't even give me one of her big, loud kisses. Her kisses are corny, but I miss them.

So far A.J. and Charlie were playing along, even though they both knew she was my mother.

They took A.J. limping away to see a doctor ("You did right, but I hope your family will be all right, too," he said to Dan as he left the room) and someone else was off asking Charlie more questions.

Mom took me into another room, saying she wanted to ask me some things, since she knew me. "We want to get him out of here and back to his parents," she added.

"I don't know if he can go back," Gravlox said. "Think of everything he's seen."

Wouldn't he be surprised.

So now I'm in a small room with Mom, with the radio playing, and she has to pretend she's calming me down before she asks a bunch of official questions. Someone is supposed to come in and take notes. But now that I know she's okay, I want to get out to the bridge, to make sure they don't hurt the timeship.

Instead of questions, Mom is giving me what's probably classified information: A few years ago, Gravlox accidentally created a WOMPER-like reaction that tore a hole in spacetime. It's possible that the explosion that sent Mom back in time fused with the one Gravlox created, sending WOMPERs back with her . . . right into Gravlox's lab in Berkeley. He was doing his own early particle research, testing theories about relativity and how nothing, really, is quite what it seems, and he created a mini-tear between dimensions. The same way

Thea's mom did back in Alexandria with her crystals and light splitting.

Gravlox successfully repeated the experiment here, in the secrecy of the redesigned fort. This new tear in spacetime hovers in the fort's central courtyard area. "But it seems to be growing, Eli. They can't control it, and they're not really sure what it is they have. They just know that stuff keeps sporadically popping out of thin air. That's how those white antlers first showed up.

"I try to do my own tests on the side, with the limited equipment they have. Everyone's scared, Eli. Nobody knows where any of this is leading—atom bombs, time warps, the war itself."

"But we know, Mom." I hear thumps and booms outside. I think they're shooting at Clyne's ship, and I'm getting really antsy. "The good guys win the war, right? The Nazis lose." At least that's one less thing she has to worry about, or that we have to discuss.

"We don't know if that's true anymore, Eli,

if that's still the way it happens. Everything's different now. History isn't the same."

"There's a dinosaur up on the Golden Gate Bridge!" It's Gravlox, who's just stuck his head into the room. "Do you think he came through our time portal?"

"No!" I blurt out. "He came from the flying time-ship up there. He's just a kid who wants to finish his schoolwork, but no one will leave him alone. I have to get out and help him before he gets hurt."

Gravlox blinks at me a moment. Another series of booms come from overhead. Then he looks at my mom. "Who did you say this young man was again, Margarite?"

"He's my son, Samuel."

These hundred-year-old rooms are like little brick caves, cold and damp and dark, and ours becomes so quiet that every sound outside is suddenly amplified. I'm looking up at my mother. She always was pretty cool.

"Well . . . did he just come through the portal, like you did?" Mom just shakes her head.

"But how—?" His second question never gets answered. The angry sergeant bursts in. "Hey, doc! You know somebody name Eli?"

"No," Gravlox says. "Should I?"

"Got a call from upstairs that the Martian lizard speaks English! And he's askin' for an 'Eli.' Already got two soldiers taken off the bridge to see a medic, thinkin' they're goin' crazy. I say we give the order to shoot and figure this all out later."

"Don't do that," I tell him. "I'm Eli."

For the second time in five minutes, the room goes completely silent.

Chapter Seventeen

Eli: Midnight Clear

December 24, 1941 C.E.

A group of us rush out the center gates of Fort Point, heading to the stairs built in the side of the hill that leads up to the Golden Gate Bridge.

I stop and look up. If the situation wasn't so scary, it would be strangely beautiful: the blue-white blaze of searchlights, the flashing red of dozens of sirens, the deep orange of the bridge itself, with the time-ship—I don't know how else to put it—*dancing* around it all. The ship is glowing, too, as if the craft itself were absorbing all those lights and shining them back out, only with the colors mixed differently.

The vessel swings under the bridge, then over it, then tips a little to *whoosh* through the two towers. Is it showing off, or searching for something?

"Why are we holding our fire, sir?" one of the soldiers nervously asks the sergeant.

"The brass are already on the phone to Washington, Private. It's out of our hands, and I don't like it. I say we blast the thing before it goes into the city."

"Maybe the ship just wants to protect—" and the sergeant is already glaring at me before I finish the sentence—"the dinosaur up there."

"You know, I'm not completely convinced you're as innocent as you make out, kid." *Kid* again.

A couple more soldiers fall in to our group. Another one passes us, heading down to the fort, pointing to something wrong with his rifle or the buttons on his overcoat.

"Probably just scared," the sergeant mutters. "Who cares if it's a spaceship? An enemy's an enemy."

We trudge up the steps, get waved past all the barricades, and I finally see my Saurian friend.

Clyne is surrounded by soldiers. He's alone in the center of a circle of guns, all pointed right at him. His arms are raised and he's slowly turning around, looking at all the weapons, and maybe—can this be right?—shaking.

"Earth Orange hello! *Kkt!* Don't shoot! Homework's not turned in yet!" He's trying to look at each one of them in the eye. Maybe he figures that way they won't be so scared, or so likely to shoot.

Gravlox turns to the sergeant. "The space-being asked for Eli, and Eli's here. Shouldn't we try to use him first?"

Grudgingly, I'm allowed to walk up and "attempt to communicate with the scaly invader," as the sergeant puts it. "But if he makes a move, we're gonna tell you to hit the deck, and we're gonna open fire, whether Washington likes it or not."

I fight the urge to stick up my arms again, with all the weapons around, and concentrate on keeping my hands in my pockets as I walk down the roadway. Now it's just me and Clyne alone in the middle of all that firepower.

I notice that the time-ship has stopped doing loop-de-loops and has pulled up, hovering alongside the bridge.

Without the explosions, I can hear music. One of these old, funky olive-green Army cars must have a radio on. Christmas music. Tinkly, in the distance. "It Came upon a Midnight Clear."

"Many heartfelt *k-k-kh!* greetings, Eli," Clyne says in what I can only describe as a dinosaur whisper, which has a lot more breath behind it than any whisper I could come up with. "Being an outlaw here is *sk-tkt!* somewhat nerve-sparking. Plus all the many projectile weapons."

"Are you okay, Clyne? How have you been?"

"Basically well. Caught in nets, kept solitary in a zoo *pp-pp-kk!* and watching the high, sad cost of war readiness in large caves. Much *tng-ga!* material for class report. Enough for two full academic terms, really. And you, friend?"

"I found my mom and met Joe DiMaggio, but it's not working out like I thought. It's getting hard to remember that some people just live their lives in straight lines. You know, from beginning to end."

"Impossible! Time doesn't move in a line like that."

"Don't get any closer, kid! Hold it right there!" the sergeant shouts at me through a bullhorn.

It is a pretty bad time for me and Clyne to be discussing physics. I have to get my friend out of this jam. "You've got to come with me, Clyne. Slowly. Before they really hurt you."

"But, Eli, we have come to *k-k-k-kt!* rescue you."

I'm suddenly aware that "Midnight Clear" is still playing, but it seems to be going on for a ridiculously long time, and I realize I'm not listening to a radio at all. It's the ship.

The ship is humming.

"'We?' Who's with you, Clyne? It's not—"

The humming changes in tone, and an opening appears in the craft. Thea slowly sticks her head out.

Half the guns swerve around to aim at her.

"HOLD YOUR FIRE!" the sergeant screams. He comes running up to me, a pistol in his hand aimed right at Clyne. "What is going on here, and why are these people invading the United States!? Who is that girl?"

"Sir . . . sir . . . it's not what you think."

"These . . . these *individuals* will either agree to be taken into custody and turn their ship over or we commence firing. Aiming to kill."

"Sir, I just don't think firing these kinds of weapons will work. Not on the ship."

I can't tell if he looks terrified or more enraged. "Is that a *threat*?"

"Eli?" It's Mom. She's come up with Gravlox. "What's happening? Who is that girl?"

Thea is becoming quite popular. "She's . . . her name is Thea. She's from Earth."

"You know her?" the sergeant demands.

"Yeah."

"How?"

"Is it because . . . from when you were . . . ?" Mom leaves the question unfinished, mainly so the sergeant won't pick up on the missing time-traveling part, but Gravlox must get it, because he's slowly nodding.

"Yeah," I say, "before I found you." I point to my two friends. "They want to take me home."

Mom looks over at Thea again, who waves at us—very carefully. "She looks nice."

"Mom!"

I don't even think before I say it. Gravlox already knows Margarite's my mother—it's the sergeant's wide eyes I'm worried about now.

"I think," the sergeant hisses through clenched teeth, "somebody owes me a big explanation. Especially when Washington gets on the phone in the next few minutes to chew my butt out for not blasting that ship to bits!"

"You don't need to blast them," I tell him. "You just need . . . you just need to let them go. And me, too. And her." I point to my mom.

"What!?" My mom and the sergeant speak in unison. But it's Mom who pulls me aside.

"Eli! What are you doing?"

"We can go back, Mom. All of us! On their ship. It's way easier than just shooting through the Fifth Dimension like a cannonball. Trust me."

"I can't go back, Eli. Not now. Not yet."

"Why not? We can just leave and let them have their history."

"But it's our history, too, Eli. Don't you see? And if it starts unraveling too fast, if they invent time travel too soon, if it gets used as a weapon . . . Somebody has to stay here. The things that happen between now and the time you're born are awful enough—your father knows I can't let them get any worse."

"Then when will you ever come back to Dad? To me?"

Suddenly the time-ship's version of "Midnight Clear" seems to be pounding in my ears, and it feels like everyone in the world is staring at me and my mom—even though it's only everyone on the bridge.

"I *can't* yet, Eli. I wouldn't be any kind of parent to you at all if I let the world get even more wrecked than it already is. Please try to understand that."

Mom wipes her eye, and I'm thinking there still might be some way to figure this out—convince her to go, convince the soldiers not to shoot at Clyne or Thea, and get us all on that ship, but before I can even think *how,* something unpredictable happens.

Fort Point explodes.

At least, a chunk of it does, and right then, the tension snaps. Bullets are whizzing everywhere—I think I see Gravlox get hit in the arm—bazookas tear off chunks of the bridge railing and the suspension cables as they try to blast the ship, and I land hard, cracking my knee as Mom pulls me down to the pavement. It's like we're in a war.

Well, I guess we are.

I don't hear "Midnight Clear" anymore, but instead a loud sound like chanting and moaning combined. From the ship, which rotates upward, then tilts on its side again. Thea's trying to get to Clyne, to both of us, but she can't get low enough.

A few of the shots hit the craft, but it seems to absorb the explosive force, though its color gets darker and darker each time, and it starts to wobble.

Clyne is jumping around. "Ouch! Mammals! Stop!" he yells. He looks like one of those guys in an old cowboy movie being made to skip and dance when the bad guys shoot around his feet. I feel sorry for him, and worried, and then mad that I can't help.

And then I watch in horror as my friend jumps over the side of the bridge.

"Clyne!" I jump up, but Mom pulls me back down.

When I look up, the time-ship's disappeared, and so have Clyne and Thea.

Chapter Eighteen

Eli: Fixing Time

December 24, 1941 C.E.

"The fort, come on." Mom prods me to follow her down the stairs before everyone's attention turns back from the vanished ship.

Below, one of the fort walls has been ripped open, and we can see smoke billowing out. Mom is in a panic to see if the time-rip is still contained.

"Whether it was the geometry of the walls, or some element in the bricks, or the weather, or the soil, I don't know, Eli. But something kept Samuel's WOMPER-reaction contained inside the fort."

"So the whole fort was like a giant version of Dad's time spheres?"

"More or less." She seems distracted. I can't blame her.

The explosion was Rolf's work. He must've been the "scared soldier" who waved to us as he headed toward the fort. A surviving witness with blood running down his face described him yelling something about Hitler as he jumped straight into the time-rip. He was holding a pair of antlers.

Seconds later, the bomb went off.

"If the whole thing's destroyed now, Mom, you can come home. There's nothing to keep watch over."

"The time-rip's invisible, Eli. The only way to know how far the field has spread is to watch its effects. For all we know, anything from Civil War veterans to cavemen could start popping up anywhere in San Francisco. But what's worse is *he's* out there now."

"Yeah. Rolf."

"He could be trying to change history, to

force it in some different direction, right this moment. Things are spinning even more out of control, Eli. I can't come home."

The smoke is getting in my nose, making my eyes watery. Mom dabs my face with her sleeve.

"Someone has to go back after him," she adds in a quieter voice. "The portal here seems to be flowing back to ancient Britain at the moment, based on the things coming out at this end."

"Like the antlers?"

"Yes."

"And you want me to go after him?"

"No. You should return to your father."

"But you sent this!" I hold up the note on Fairmont letterhead with the word *help* on it.

"I was feeling desperate that day. I wanted to come home. I still do. But I can't. That was like a message in a bottle, Eli—I wasn't really sure where it would wind up. Look at the ink."

She lightly touches the paper.

"After the explosion, when I regained

consciousness in Samuel's lab, I still had most of the things that were stuck in my pockets. Including the pen I'd been using."

I know the one she means: a carved wooden pen, shaped to look like a double helix, those two long twisted strands of DNA. Dad gave it to her as a gift when they were dating. I always considered it one of those details that just confirms your parents are, in fact, a little weird. She reaches into her pocket and takes the pen out now.

"I don't show it here much, because no one knows what a DNA strand looks like yet. But I wrote the note with it. I'm working on a theory that objects hold a kind of energy or memory of a place or time—and can help take you there."

"But that won't be any use to you in finding Rolf." Now it's my turn. I take the chronocompass out of my pocket. "This can help me find him, though. And you can go back home."

"What is it?"

"A prototype Dad was working on. Like a steering wheel through time."

"Dr. Franchon?" One of the soldiers comes up, and I hide the compass in my hand. He points to me. "I have orders to hold the boy here until everything gets straightened out. A lot of people have a lot of questions for him. And for you, too."

"Where are you taking him?"

He doesn't answer that question. "Sorry, ma'am. You'll have to say goodbye here."

Mom bends over and whispers to me. "I should be the one to fix this. I helped make this mess. You need to go home."

"We all need to go home."

She takes out a slip of paper. "I was hoping I could get this to your father." With her DNA pen, she quickly scribbles something else on it, then slips it in my pocket. "I love you more than anything, Eli."

"Sorry, Doctor." The soldier is eager to get going.

"I want to go with him," she tells the soldier. "Wherever you're taking him."

If I stick around, they'll keep asking me questions that will get harder and harder to answer. But I don't know if I'm going home, either. Mom's right about getting history unstuck, or back on track. Especially if Rolf Royd is out there trying to change things.

Mom is arguing with the soldier, and while she does, I take the cap out of my pocket and begin rubbing the Thickskin off, right around the area that DiMaggio signed for me—right over the *D.B.*

I start to feel the cap tingling against my skin. I pull it on.

"I love you, too," I tell her. And in case it's already morning, I add "Merry Christmas." By the time she and the soldier turn around, I'm gone.

Hopefully she'll worry less, thinking I have the compass. I didn't want to tell her it all fused together on my trip back here.

I'm really not sure where I'll wind up.

Chapter Nineteen

Eli: Lake Arrivals

Somewhere in Old England . . .

I'm completely soaked again.

I stagger, coughing, out of the lake and flop down. Two guys in costumes are staring at me. They both have beards. One is wearing . . . not a crown, exactly, but a ring around his head, with a small jewel in the center over his forehead. His robes and vests are kind of greasy, his hair's a little matted, and he's holding a sword.

"Merlin, is this one of yours?" the jewel wearer asks.

Merlin? Couldn't be. Then the one asking the question is probably . . .

"Arthur?" I sputter it more than say it.

I guess they aren't costumes after all.

"What a bold lad, to appear out of the ether and address his king like an old friend."

I can't worry about the ground rules for talking to some ancient king right now—the trip across the Fifth Dimension has made me sick, and the waterlogged Seals cap is already beginning to tingle on my head, but I'm not ready to be jerked back into the time stream yet.

I was lucky enough to get here without being able to use the chrono-compass. I don't have anything from King Arthur's England that would have taken me back here. Rolf is the one with the White Stag's antlers. . . .

Which he scratched me with. Is there something in my blood now? Some secondhand body-memory of this place? Do I have stag WOMPERs in my veins?

I don't know. Thinking about it gives me a headache, along with the tingling. I snatch the cap off and toss it toward Merlin for safekeeping. "Could you hold that, please?" Then I bend over and throw up.

"A most peculiar lad, indeed. Methinks he mocks his king."

I glance up between heaves to see that Merlin has my cap in his hands, and he's chuckling a little as he examines it. Then he points to a spot over the lake, where I appeared.

"Did you see how he came out of the very air like that, Arthur? You may not be *his* king at all."

"Then who is he? Is this one of your tricks, you senile wizard, to try and make me keep this bloody sword?"

"No one can make you keep Excalibur, Arthur, if you no longer feel worthy of it."

"Bah! Another of your tricks, you goblin, with your prodding words. This has nothing to do with my *worth.*"

I can still remember, before WOMPERs and Mom's disappearance, that I had a regular life. Part of that included seeing my mom and dad fight sometimes. I can still remember how ridiculous I thought some of their arguments were, how I could see their fights starting, like a long, slow fuse on a cherry bomb. But they couldn't, or wouldn't, be able to stop or see what they were doing, and soon they'd be shouting at each other. Eventually someone would slam a door, and there'd be silence for a while until someone made up.

Merlin and Arthur sound like they're starting one of those married-people fights right now. Over Excalibur. The Dragon Sword.

"In fact, you haunted, spell-casting *toad,* I cannot wait to hurl this infernal scrap of metal into the water right now and let *her* worry about keeping it out of the hands of every throne-smitten young buck who comes wandering down the road."

"Apparently, Arthur, she's not waiting too much longer to accept the privilege." I look over the lake, in the direction Merlin is nodding.

There's a woman hovering there, and she's practically *naked*—the only thing covering her is the long, flowing hair floating around her body.

Who is she? How does she stay out there like that? She's waving now at Arthur, at Merlin.

"The Lady of the Lake will disappear, Arthur. She won't wait forever." Merlin doesn't seem very concerned. He's still giving my cap the once-over.

Maybe the Lady of the Lake is time-tangled, too. Maybe there have always been people like me, throughout history, who can fade in and out of different "whens"—and maybe that explains a lot of ghosts and spirits and magic beings.

Maybe I'm not the only Danger Boy.

Then she winks. Right at me. I swear it. And then she's gone.

The water where's she vanished is still churning.

"The lad has scared her off."

Lad. At least it's not *kid.* Lad, like Laddy. King Arthur and Laddy.

I'm in a cartoon.

But cartoons are supposed to be fun. And not so sad.

I finally feel less nauseated, and I stand up. The water in the lake begins bubbling again, and I turn, thinking maybe she's come back. But it's not her.

It's dragon-jerk Rolf.

He's surprised to find himself in water, just like I was, and starts splashing around, letting go of the antlers.

"Look, Merlin," King Arthur says, pointing at them. "The horns of the White Stag are back."

"They're sinking in the lake. With the new boy."

"Well, do something magic to get them back! Send this other airy lad"—Arthur points at me—"into the lake to fetch them!"

"It's not my place, your *majesty,* to go ordering boy warlocks around."

"What if it's a magic attack? A trick by Morgan Le Fey? It's your job to protect your king, Merlin."

"Pardon me, sire. I thought you were done being king."

As Merlin and the king bicker, Rolf turns out to be a pretty good swimmer. He heads toward us and eventually pulls himself ashore.

He stands and leans over to spit out water, and I think he's going to be sick, too. But it's worse than that. Time travel's harder on him: His hair is all white.

Though that doesn't stop him, once he catches his breath, from declaring we're all his prisoners.

Then he asks Arthur to hand over the sword—Excalibur, the Dragon Sword—in the name of the Reich.

Worst of all, King Arthur does.

Chapter Twenty

Eli: Dragon Hunt

Somewhere in Old England . . .

"You cannot give away Excalibur!" Merlin has lost the amused look on his face. "You've gone batty after all! It must be hidden away! For the next true king to claim!"

"Oh, you were right, magician. I'm done being king. So let him have it. Who cares? He's claiming it in the name of this . . . 'Ryck,' this King Ryck, whoever that is."

Rolf the showoff keeps trying to lift the sword over his head but seems to be having a hard time controlling it. "I . . ." he huffs out,

"Rolf Royd . . . do hearby claim this magic object in the name of the Reich . . ."

"You see?" King Arthur says to his wizard. "I've never even heard of this Ryck. They're coming out of the woodwork, now that they think I'm weak."

"You cannot transfer power to this boy!"

"Don't be so alarmed"—Arthur points at Rolf—"he can hardly lift it." The sword seems to be pulling him, like someone tugged along by a dog on a leash. "The lad will have to give up in a few minutes."

But Rolfie seems determined. "And in the name of the *Drachenjungen* . . ."

"Did he say something about dragons?" Arthur asks. "Is he going to hunt dragons with it?"

Rolfie-the-hunter grips the sword, but it moves on its own, spinning him around. "I *would* like another dragon hunt," Arthur says.

"You have already killed them all, sire," Merlin says with a trace of scorn.

"Ah. Right." Just as he was starting to

brighten up, the king looks depressed again. Then he turns to me. "I suppose you will want a turn with the sword, too, young pup?"

"No. But you can't let him have it, Mr. . . . King Arthur, sir. He wants to use its power to do bad things to people."

"Boy, I, too, once believed I could stop bad things from happening in the world."

"Oh, really! Must you always be so glum? Ever since Queen Guinevere left"—and I realize that Merlin is addressing this comment to me—"he has been so hopelessly bleak. That's the danger of love. Look"—his attention shifts back to Arthur—"this boy is right. You're being absurd. We have to stop this before *that* one learns how to wield it."

At that moment, the sword goes flying out of Rolf's hands, like a hammer toss, and plows tip-first into the ground, just missing my foot.

"There, you see, Merlin? That blade is like a wild horse. You told me the sword itself chooses who wields it. Which makes it practically useless, anyway."

"You never felt that way before."

"I have changed, old wizard. You pretend not to see it."

But I'm staring at Rolf, who seems to have changed a lot, too, even if he is still a dragon jerk. Not only is his hair white, but the skin around his face is . . . patchy. Something happened to him out in the Fifth Dimension. He might have landed somewhere else and stayed there for years, for all I know, before he wound up here. Which could explain his late arrival. There are no guarantees of anything coming out the way you think it will when you duck in and out of time. And something certainly has gone wrong for Mr. White Hair.

But his attitude hasn't changed any.

"Look out!" I yell. Rolf has reached under his waterlogged jacket and pulled out the pistol strapped to his leg.

But Merlin's on top of it, and just as Rolf's gun *CRACKS!*, so does a wand from under Merlin's robe.

The bullet stops in midair. And so does Rolf.

Or at least his legs do. He can't move them. But his eyes are open wide.

"What is that?" Merlin asks, stepping up to examine the bullet more closely. "You had better move, Arthur. This little sword pellet is heading right toward you, and I can't hold it forever. I've warned you, magic's fading from the world."

"Then talk to these boys who seem to know how to appear out of thin air! And let the little flying dagger come, you overgrown leprechaun. I am tired of fighting boys who think they need to be king. Let the little pellet come, and let me rest."

Merlin shakes his head at me. "Many seasons back, the queen and one of the king's knights thought they were in love with each other. And I have had to listen to Arthur go on about it ever since. It's not as if people aren't sorry, but it scarcely matters to him. The king would be gone a year or more at a time in those days. And the queen was young! What did he expect? 'Tis hard on people to be apart like that."

"Yeah," I tell him. "I know."

The lake is starting to churn again. "You see, Merlin. The Lady isn't finished with us yet," Arthur says. "The time has come to be rid of this infernal thing." He pulls Excalibur out of the ground.

"Such a waste," Merlin sighs to me. "I should never have agreed to conjure her again. He is determined to give his Dragon Sword to the Lady of the Lake."

"But why?"

"So she can hide it. I am afraid he really is through being king. I am afraid that this is the end, at last, of Arthur's kingdom. Of Camelot."

"But you'll always know where Excalibur is, right?" I ask. "No matter where she puts it?"

"She will not hide it in another place, but another time, lad. I don't know where—or when—she comes from. 'Tis a time-altering spell that allows her to appear at the lake."

But time isn't being altered by the Lady of the Lake.

It's the Saurian ship that appears.

Merlin is so shocked, he drops his wand. The bullet is freed from its spell and goes whizzing right past Arthur—who luckily has moved to get a better view of the craft.

Rolf is cut loose, too, and falls to the ground, before getting up and bolting away into the forest.

"Hey!" I yell after him. But I don't want to chase him. I want to see if my friends are all right first.

After circling around overhead, the ship lands in a grass clearing inside a ring of oaks.

The entrance panel slides open, and Thea once again pops her head out. She looks around, a little cautiously—to make sure no one is shooting at her this time—then sees me with King Arthur and Merlin.

"A most remarkable sorceress!" Merlin exclaims.

She says something, but I can't understand

it. The heavily accented English of Merlin and Arthur is bad enough—but without a lingo-spot, I don't have a chance of figuring out Thea.

Just like in Alexandria, she dabs a little of her own spot behind my ear. It tingles, too, like a milder version of my Seals cap.

"I said," she repeats, "that I am tired of being called a sorceress."

"I understood you the first time!" Merlin says, coming up to us. "I recognize that tongue from desert lands."

Thea smiles at him, then turns her attention back to me. "And you, Eli the Boy Wizard, are a hard person to track down."

"Well, at least I've been on the same planet the whole time," I tell her.

"So you *are* all wizards, then!" Merlin exclaims. "Magic *is* coming back into the world!"

"I am an astronomer," Thea says, "a mathematician, and a librarian. Who are you?"

But I cut off Merlin's answer with another

question. “Thea! If you’re here . . . then Clyne . . . when he jumped off the bridge . . . ?”

I have visions of his body floating around the ocean, winding up in some fisherman’s net, and a headline in that *Weekly Truth* paper about someone finding a sea serpent.

“At last a quiet time on Earth Orange! Let us *kk-kk-dng!* picnic here before getting back to studies!”

“He’s a hard person to track down, too,” Thea says as Clyne bounds out of the ship, “especially when he’s falling from a bridge.”

I’m so glad you’re okay, Clyne! That’s what I want to tell him, but I don’t get the chance.

“Merlin!” shouts Arthur. “Merlin you old rascal, look! Dragons live, after all! You have brought one to me and I shall have at it! Sword”—and now he’s talking to Excalibur—“good times have come back to England! *YAH-HHHH!*”

And with a roar, Arthur runs at Clyne, swinging his Dragon Sword, ready to cut my friend’s head off.

Chapter Twenty-one

Thea: Tintagel

Merlin's Time

When I glimpsed forests and no cities, I thought we could rest in this world awhile. K'lion, Eli, and I are a small society: Unmoored in time, we have seen things most people in our homelands would never believe.

Our friendship has been forged in fire and movement. We've had no time to really talk, play, or as K'lion says, "picnic."

I thought that time would be now. Instead, I find myself disoriented, surrounded by trees in a thick, dark woodland, the likes of which I never saw near Alexandria.

I ran into these woods thinking I could keep K'lion from being hunted by this king, whoever he is. Alexandria is—was a port city where news of the world came to us regularly. And though I know of both Celts and Britons, I have never heard of this "Arthur." Of course, I am not precisely sure *when* this is, either.

I entered the forest, side by side with Eli. We were both yelling that K'lion was not a dragon. But the king was far ahead of us, chasing our friend, who at least outpaced his pursuer with great leaps.

Eli seemed to think he could make the king call off the hunt if he could only explain about K'lion, but the king's enthusiasm made it hard to catch up. And then, quite suddenly, Eli was gone.

I do not know how, precisely. Perhaps all forests shift like this as you move through them, with paths closing off and new ones opening up, so that you can never be sure exactly where you are. They are disorienting. Alexandria's boulevards, its harbors, and the desert vistas outside the city were much easier to navigate.

"Don't be so hard on yourself, sorceress. 'Tis a magic wood. I designed it so that most would lose their way."

There was no warning, no sound—he just appeared. Merlin.

His sleeves were wet, and he was holding a set of white antlers.

"I am trying to keep your king from killing my friend," I told him. "If I can ever find them."

"Unfortunately," Merlin said with a shrug, "only the king can find his way through this wood. We nonroyals usually have to wait for the cry of a magical creature, like a dragon, to guide us out. But I think your dragon man will be safe. Arthur doesn't quite have the blood lust he once did."

He ran a finger over the antlers. "He hunted the White Stag with his bare hands and cut the antlers off. I should never have told him the horns have power. Because the power never lasts, and the greater sadness is an empty forest."

"Thinking woods, magic horns, and spells! Are you really standing here talking to me, wizard, or is this another of your tricks!" The words were no sooner out of my mouth than I stopped, stunned to realize how much I sounded like Brother Tiberius, the falsely pious monk who stirred a riot against my mother and caused her death. He routinely accused Mother and me of witchcraft.

"Do not doubt yourself, child. You see what you see." He was pointing behind me.

I turned and peered through a clearing, which spread out to bluffs overlooking the sea. Towering above the cliffs were the ruins of a once-great palace.

"How could we be so near the sea? I didn't hear it, or even smell it . . . and I always smell the water," I said. And then softer, more for my ears than his, "My mother used to call me 'Mermaid.'"

"Ah, mermaids. Yes. I miss them," Merlin said. "All of ours left some time ago. Swam off toward the Viking territories, I think—the shelter of all those deep fjords. I expect they're terribly cold." He shook the antlers again. "I believe I shall hang these up in the Great Hall. Why not come with me, lass? Perhaps your friends will come along."

"People still live there?"

"Just Arthur and me. Even the servants have left now. Tintagel, we call it," he said, walking toward it. "And it was great in its day!" he yelled over his shoulder.

I ran after him. "You walked off without me!"

"You are free to follow or not."

"Couldn't you use magic to force me along?" I asked him, again sounding too much like Tiberius.

"Oh, that would be a bad use of the craft, indeed. Besides, 'tis you should be doing magic."

"Why do you say that?" My suspicion flared anew.

"You will see. I sense a rather interesting and profound future for you, if not always an enviable one."

"What do you mean?"

"'Tis a journey you will have to make yourself, m'lady. That's really all I know. Partial glimpses make Arthur crazy, too. Look."

We stood at the entrance to the stone palace. It had been mighty once, towering over the landscape.

"Did you have a library and gardens . . . and a zoo?" I asked, remembering the palace grounds in Alexandria.

"We had everything, lass—Arthur and his queen, the Knights of the Round Table, the citizens of this kingdom. We were rich, with stories to tell and a purpose in the world."

"What happened?"

"It's hard to say, exactly. Not everyone shares the same purpose. Not everyone's heart can sustain joy. Humans tend to feel restless without a good fight." He gave me a small smile. "There were wars. Come, let us go to the Great Hall."

Inside, the castle was drafty and dark. Torches still lit many of the halls; fires burned in hearths in many of the rooms. In some ways, it felt as people had just left, and—despite the breeze and holes in the walls—might return shortly. A feeling of having just missed something.

"The Great Hall, lady."

"My proper name is Thea."

"Named for the moon and shining light. Perfect."

I looked around. We were in a small chamber. There was a fire in the hearth, two hard wooden beds covered in furs and skins, some large, rough-hewn chairs, and a couple of tables: One held the implements of science—maps of the constellations, hourglasses, compasses, and the like.

The other table had the implements of dining, if *dining* wasn't too fine a word for it:

bread rinds, half-empty wine goblets, chewed animal bones, and more. Odors drifted from the unwashed platters.

"Yes, the Great Hall. Or at least, the only hall actually used by the castle's current occupants."

On the wall opposite the beds hung a tapestry. Picking up a candle, I walked over to it: There was King Arthur next to a queen, several knights, dozens of retainers, children, animals, banners, and in the background, Merlin himself.

It must have taken a terribly long time to weave.

"The rest are all gone now," Merlin said.

"Why?" I asked.

"The castle became almost impossible to defend. Somebody always wanted to take it, to come after the great king. And if they weren't coming after Arthur or trying to ransack Tintagel, then Arthur and his knights were off seeking impossible things. Which made it even harder for those left behind to protect themselves."

"What things?"

"The Holy Grail. Perfect love. Things humans aren't meant to have." Merlin raised the antlers to the wall, evidently looking for a place to hang them.

"These people didn't love each other?" I was intrigued with all the faces in the tapestry. The weaver made them all seem . . . very alive.

"Oh, they did, lass. The Round-Table Knights. Arthur and his Guinevere. But none of it is perfect. 'Tis all only human. Things are never quite as good as imagined. Nor as bad."

"Have you heard of a place called Peenemünde?" I asked, turning to face him.

"Why do you ask?"

I told him about everything I'd seen there—the wraithlike people working as slaves, the weapons and rockets they were building, the brutality of the overseers, of the Reich—their soldiers, their officers, and yes, the scientists—who ran it.

And then I showed him the picture of the mother and child, which I still had in my tunic.

Merlin held the image, then softly closed his eyes before handing it back to me.

"What am I to make of your future, child?"

"It isn't mine. Well, perhaps it is now." I slipped the picture back into my robes. "But those horrors have yet to happen. Peenemünde is built in times to come. Isn't there a way to stop it?"

"That is the same thing I wondered, stripling, about the battles that destroyed our kingdom."

"Couldn't your magic end them?"

"For magic to really work, Thea, you have to let it in. You have to be open to it, the same way that you, as a scientist, have to be open."

"But science uses logic and deduction. Magic feeds on fear and superstition."

"Both lead to enchantment, if you follow them to the place where the world's greatest mysteries awe you." With that, he held out his hand—he was now holding some of the plasmechanical skin from the time-vessel.

It was then I realized the antlers were

already hanging on the wall. Merlin folded up his hand inside his robe and turned to tend the fire.

"We could bring magic back into the world, Thea. I need an apprentice, someone to teach. Before it's too late."

"Before what's too late?"

"Before the world is set on a course that brings us Peenemünde—and all that comes with it."

Remain here to learn magic? From an old wizard? I imagine Mother would be properly horrified.

"My friends aren't safe yet. They are my family now. What about them?"

"After your friends are safe, of course. Decide then."

"And how do you know they will be? There was some other boy here when K'lion—when the dragon man and I landed. Who was that?"

"In recounting your journey, you mentioned the word *Reich*, did you not? I believe that other boy comes from the world of Peenemünde. And wishes to acquire more power, to spread harm."

The news hit me like a full beam from Pharos.

"Then take me out of here, back through your magical woods, and show me how to find my friends!"

"Very well. But I have learned there is much less you can do to protect them than you might imagine."

"I have always prided myself on a very active imagination."

Then a loud, unearthly scream came to my ears, freezing me where I stood.

"What was that?" I whispered.

"That," Merlin answered, rising from the fireplace, "sounded very much like the battle yell of a dragon."

Chapter Twenty-two

Clyne: Ungarth

After Dragons

What strange Saurian music. The notes looked like an ancient war cry, from the times before Cacklaw. I sounded it out myself, from the transcription on the wall. What an odd and eerie noise. I wonder how often such a cry was used. And on a planet such as this, once home to both Saurians and mammals, was such a sound meant as a warning? As tribal comfort? A way to grieve?

The cave I'd found through sheer whiffery. I was surprised—shocked, even—to find vaguely familiar Saurian odors wafting into my nasal ramps as I raced through this forest.

Despite the medium-grade danger I was in from the mammal-king who wanted to slay me, I decided to follow the scent. This was the first real evidence I had of another Saurian presence on Earth Orange. And that evidence led me to the nest-home of Ungarth.

At least, I believe it was pronounced "Ungarth." The pictographs on the wall are in ancient Saurian, and in a strange dialect at that. I was sounding them out—singing them—as I read along. According to the record, this is their story:

A type of Saurian, native to this planet, did survive their otherwise disastrous encounter with a meteor, an incident known on other Earths as the Great Sky Hammer. It seems, strangely, to have occurred—with varying degrees of severity—in numerous parallel dimensions at once (a fact that bears further research).

On Earth Orange, the results were shell-shattering: Mammals surprisingly evolved to become the dominant class of species. Dominant, at least, in terms of their impact on the planet. The insects are far more numerous.

As for Ungarth's people—he calls them Saurish Folk, a term that tickles my imagination nodes and which I may start using—they grew and lived and prospered in secret. Ungarth didn't know the term *Homo sapiens,* which I learned while studying at the zoo with Howe and Thirty, but he describes an emerging species of "singing hunters." They invented their own weapons and wars, tales and legends, and the few Saurians they would glimpse became known as "dragons." This was possibly derived from *draghoorh,* a Saurish term for "lost one."

As their numbers dwindled, the word became a type of greeting between the Saurish.

At first, these early humans were content to live with these "dragons," but dragons, in

Ungarth's words, "need wide places to dream and roam." And with human tribes growing, there were fewer wide places available.

Eventually, human warriors would hunt these dragons as a way of proving their bravery to their own tribes. A chill ran down my backslope reading this: I was reminded of the destruction of the Bloody Tendon Wars in our own ancient history—when the meat-eaters and plant-eaters battled each other over what—or who—should be called "food."

The singing hunters pursued their Saurish prey for generations. And as my absent host wrote: "I, Ungarth, faced off with their king, Arthur, many times throughout my life. As we both grew older—and sadder—he finally managed to injure me. I had let my guard down. Arthur came in for the kill. 'Give me your worst flame, dragon. I shall still win.' I replied in his language: 'We do not have fire in our breath. That was just a trick with light and steam to impress your kind.' The exchange seemed to shock him—he held off delivering a death blow. I retreated to this small cave to lick my wounds and hide from the world. As far as I know, I am now the last of the Saurish Folk."

After that, Ungarth composed the Saurish history on the wall in front of me. When I tried singing it, the effect was startling. There was a dissonance to it. Perhaps it was a mammal-like cultural influence on the Saurians of Earth Orange. In which case, I am left to wonder: What effect did the dragons have on the humans in exchange?

Now *there* would be a thesis topic unique in the history of our school!

I don't know how much longer Ungarth lived. His song cycle ended with a chant about returning to the "mists of the first valley." All his artifacts were still in the cave. My thought was to bring many of them home for further study, in the vessel piloted by Thea.

There was, for example, a simple fitted skull-screen, for protective wear. When I put it on my cranium, I must have looked like an actual top-stomper from an ancient round of Cacklaw. But I didn't have time to marvel at the image.

"Ungarth! 'Tis you come back to me!" It was the mammal-king, Arthur. Brandishing his sword.

"Not Ungarth, me. Ungarth died," I told him. "I'm *k-k-kt!* compiling merely extra credit. I mean no pain to you." I smiled and tried extending my forearm in the friendship gesture I had witnessed.

He nearly sliced my claws off. "The *legend* says you died, but I know I only nicked you that day. Lancelot is gone. Perceval is gone. Guinevere is gone. Knights and queens all gone. But *you,* I knew you would come back to me! And I daresay the fire's real this time."

He took a few more swipes with the blade, and in that close space I had to time my jumps to stay away from him.

"No! Fire-breathing *was* a *kt!* trick! No pain aimed!" Maybe if he thought I *was* Ungarth, he would hear better.

"Doesn't . . . *matter,*" King Mammal grunted,

swinging and managing to just cut into the end of my tail. His pain *was* aimed. I'm glad I *wasn't* Ungarth, if this was his constant game-cycle with the king. "I had to slay dragons to keep the people happy. I was king! It was expected. And now all that's left me is to prove I was ever king at all."

"I believe you! I believe you!" But I wasn't the one he needed to prove it to. I have discovered that the inner-face is fragile among Earth Orange mammals. I have a theory this may be connected to the atmospheric gases here, but I've had no time to run field experiments.

He swung at me again, and I was forced into an improvised Cacklaw move—bouncing off the cave wall, flipping over in the air, landing behind the king, then spinning around to lash him with my tail.

The tail-whip sent him tumbling over, the sword flying from his hands. I picked it up to keep it away from him and immediately noticed a vibration that pulsed through the weapon.

King Mammal—who now looked very sad indeed—stared up at me from the ground. "I suppose it's your turn to end the game, eh, Ungarth?"

"We can play *skt!* something else, instead," I offered.

"Why don't we play Give the Sword to the Dragon Youth?" It wasn't the king's voice. I turned and saw them at the cave entrance: My friend Eli, held prisoner by the other time-roaming boy. He had his gun pointed at Eli's head.

"Hi, Clyne," Eli said, sounding both regretful and irked. "I heard your cry. Unfortunately, Rolf here was waiting for me by the cave."

"Hello, friend Eli. And you, *d-dk!* Dragon Youth Rolf, should content yourself with simply Rolf. You are most definitely no dragon."

"If I bring that sword back, I am a dragon, wolf, lion—whatever I wish. The Fuerher himself will reward me. Thanks to your stumbling through time with that ship, I can make this assignment more glorious than a suicide mission. Give me the weapon, and I will let the little American go."

"Brash boy! You cannot handle Excalibur!" the king spat. "The sword will eat you up! For once, Ungarth is right: You are no dragon!"

"The boy for the sword." Rolf No-Dragon looked right at me. He clicked his gun apparatus, preparing to cause Eli terrible harm. On purpose.

I threw the blade down on the floor of the cave. "Let my friend go. Please, mammal."

"We shall see who the most fearsome creature here is," the Rolf said as he picked up the blade. "You see, old king, I am perfectly able to—"

The sudden effect was like a terrible case of herk-jitters. The sword swung the Rolf around so much he looked like a Saurian losing an argument with his tail about which direction to go. Eli ran over to me, as much to be free of Rolf No-Dragon as to get out of the way of the erratically moving blade.

"Give me back my sword!" roared the king,

diving for the boy. Although the Rolf tried to aim the weapon in the king's general direction, it was the boy who was flung at the monarch by the dancing blade. But he kept enough of a grip on the weapon to nick the king by chance as he and the sword went sailing by.

"Excalibur!" King Mammal yelled, seemingly more outraged than injured. He sunk to the floor, like a rear-guard ace in Cacklaw who realizes all at once that the other clan is about to overrun him.

"Excalibur," the king hissed. "Excalibur has *hurt* me."

As the king's red blood dripped onto the ground, I wondered what Ungarth would think to know that Arthur was now bleeding in his cave, too.

Chapter Twenty-three

Eli: Dragon Sword

Somewhere in Old England . . .

King Arthur's holding his arm, furious, not from the cut, which is bad enough, but at the fact that it happened with his own sword.

I'm trying to remember if Laddy ever found himself in a jam like this with Arthur in any of those old cartoons. Those cartoons, though, weren't really scary. Not the way this Rolf is genuinely, actually scary.

He's still being jerked around by Excalibur, but he won't drop it. Maybe if we just stay out of his way, he'll smash into a wall.

I wish I could've smashed him into a wall earlier.

I was lost almost as soon as I ran into the woods. Thea was next to me, then disappeared. The path I thought I was on disappeared, too. I was surrounded by trees.

I yelled, but no one yelled back. I was definitely, absolutely lost.

That was also genuinely scary.

And I might still be out there if Clyne hadn't screamed. Actually, I didn't know it was Clyne at first. Didn't know what it was. But it was the first noise beside my own voice I'd heard, and the trees suddenly opened up in the direction the sound came from—so I followed.

I heard water, then found a stream. I bent over to take a drink. Two sips later, the reflection of a cave appeared in the water. When I was looking straight at the same spot a moment before, I hadn't seen a thing.

I sat up, and there it was—a large opening hidden behind some vines in the high banks along the creek. And then I heard Clyne and Arthur, and it sounded like they were fighting.

But I didn't get to see their fight—I had one of my own. Rolf jumped me as I was heading inside.

"Hi, Roy Rogers!" He was almost cheerful about it as he knocked me down.

"Get off me! I'm sick of you!" I tried to punch him, but since he was on my back, I couldn't reach.

"You will have a chance to be sick of me—and the Reich—for a thousand years, little Roy!" I decided to let the "little" crack pass for now. "I knew someone would come along and want to help, acting out of cheap sentimentality," he said with a smile. "Now I have a hostage, a bargaining chip. Because everyone else will be sentimental, too. Get up!"

I felt the gun press against the base of my skull, and I rose slowly to my feet. You hate to think of someone like Rolf being both clever and patient. You just wish people who do bad things in the world would have their plans backfire every once in a while.

"Inside, let's go. The Allies' secret time-travel project ends here, hundreds of years before it begins."

"I'm not from the same war you're from!"

"We are all from the same war, Roy Rogers."

That's when we went in to see Clyne holding the sword over King Arthur.

But Rolf isn't thinking about what war he's in now. All he's thinking about is not stabbing himself in the guts with a blade he can't control.

Rolf looks like he's getting electroshock treatments, the way he's being jerked around. Finally he spins and smashes the sword against the wall of the cave, knocking it out of his hands. Instead of reaching for it, he pulls out his gun again. This time, he aims at Clyne.

"Pick it up," he tells him.

Clyne cocks his head. "Mammal weapons. No thanks."

"You can control it. You will pick the sword

up and return to the ship with me. You are from an inferior race, but I need you."

"Inferior *skkt!* race? Don't judge species-wise. First guesses can be wrong—I know. Besides, *kktng!*"—and Clyne tapped on the weird helmet he was wearing—"we were here first."

"You won't be here at all unless you pick up that sword."

"Field trip rules say no threats can be made *ch-ch-chng!* or agreed to."

"Very well."

I reach down and grab the sword handle, but it's like trying to hold a bolt of lightning, and it shoots out of my hand. The distraction is enough to turn Rolf toward me. It all happens so quickly, I'm not sure if his gun is clicking and maybe I should be dead, but I'm not. I run straight at him and plow into his stomach with my shoulder, knocking him on the ground. Maybe I should still be scared, but now all I feel is white-hot anger.

"Quit *hurting* people!" I have a rock in my

hand and I want to bash him with it, hurt him right back. "You kill families and innocent people! Mothers and babies!" I spit at him.

"It isn't killing," he answers slowly. "It's sweeping the floor."

That's it. I've never hurt anyone. Never beat anyone up before. But my mom is stuck somewhere trying to fight guys like him who are hurting *kids* on purpose, and maybe it's time one of this big punk's plans backfired after all.

"No." It's Thea. "Don't."

Rolf doesn't hesitate in the slight pause to grab his gun and pull it up point-blank. "Cheap sentimentality, Roy Rogers." I see him squeeze the trigger—

"Empty." That's Merlin.

"The little pellets inside. I transformed them into powder, over by the lake." Rolf is pulling the trigger frantically. "I pride myself on being a little useful, still," the wizard adds.

Only then does it feel safe to turn my attention away from Rolf, where I see the biggest surprise of the day.

Thea stands holding Excalibur.

"You are nothing but a bully." She has the sword pointed right at Rolf. It doesn't shake or tremble, and neither does she. "Bullies killed my mother. Bullies burned my city. I will not have my friend become a bully, too."

Now the blade is pressed against Rolf's lip, right under his nose. His eyes cross as he stares at it.

"Name your parents," she demands.

His eyes widen a little more, but he doesn't answer. "Name your parents!" And as I wonder what Thea's about to do next, it hits me: He doesn't understand her.

"She said tell her who your parents are." I'm wearing a lingo-spot, and Rolf speaks English. Thea flicks the tip of the sword under his nose. "I think you better tell her."

"Lukas and Marie," he whispers.

"Again. Like you miss them." She doesn't take any pressure off the sword. I've never seen Thea like this.

Rolf understands that order just fine. "Lukas

and Marie," he says, louder. And then adds, without being asked, "Two sisters, too. Katarina and Lisl."

"My mother's name was Hypatia," Thea tells him. "She was murdered. Eli, tell him who your parents are."

"Sandusky and—" I stop myself. I don't want to say my mom's name. Rolf would know Margarite Franchon. She was probably one of the people he was after. I didn't want him to know I was her son. "My mother disappeared after an accident."

"K'lion? Your parents?"

"Many sires and dames, *ssk!* Thea. Clutch-parents all, raising the young in groups. Kelber was special clutch-'dad' to me, passing on star lore and telling of dimension travel by nightfire. Lemny mothered sweetly, *smm!* with Cacklaw tips and legends, and fern soup for gray days with nostril ailments."

Thea keeps staring at Rolf. "There, you see? You are no different from the rest of us. You're somebody's child, too. You come from someplace. Everything you've told yourself to make yourself a bully is a lie."

I translate it for Rolf. His face changes, and, for just a moment, he almost looks like a normal teenager, instead of someone pretending to be a grownup. He doesn't say anything, doesn't move. Just lies there against the cave wall.

Having made her point, Thea throws the sword down. I see Rolf's eyes bulge a little, and his body twitches. I realize he's trying to go for the sword again but can't. He's unable to move.

"I recast the spell I had on him by the lake. He won't have use of his arms and legs for some time. This should make your prisoner easier to handle."

"Thank you, Merlin," Thea says.

The word *prisoner* lands on me with a thud. If Rolf is our prisoner, where are we supposed to take him? And what are Clyne and Thea going to do?

"I guess maybe we will need to get back to the ship," I say. There's a nod from Thea.

Merlin helps King Arthur to his feet, and with his good arm, the king lifts up Excalibur, holding it now like he's never seen it before. He keeps casting glances at Thea, and so do I.

"What?" she finally says, after being stared at so much. "He *is* a bully."

But that's not why we're looking at her. Thea acted like holding the sword was no big deal. But our stares are making her a little self-conscious. "Perhaps we should leave now."

"Would like first to take science trinkets, memory objects, and ancient-history knacks from an old friend I *snkkt!* never knew. You, King," Clyne says to Arthur, "knew him well. His name was Ungarth."

"A fierce beast. And a deadly opponent for many."

"A witness. A lastling. He had no one to share reports with. And so left one here *t-t-ttt!* on the wall."

Clyne proceeds to tell Ungarth's story as he moves along the sides of the cave, pointing at the pictures and symbols. When he finishes, Arthur seems a little shaken.

"So much of what I thought I knew . . . was wrong," he says quietly.

"I tried to tell you," Merlin says.

"Be quiet, wizard!" King Arthur snaps, then turns to Clyne. "And to you, I would like to make my amends to Ungarth. I can no longer ask his forgiveness directly."

"That mistake-mend is not mine to grant. But *tew-ptt!* I forgive you. Time journeys are unknown to you, rectifying is out of reach. So head forward now *kt-chw!* with a rephrased heart."

"Thank you," Arthur replies. "If you just said what I think you did."

"If you and Ungarth could have just *sn-kww!* played *k-kt!* Cacklaw instead of trying to kill each other, the wall report would read more kindly," Clyne says. Then he begins to gather things from around the cave.

Thea and I move to help him. "Appreciated,

friends, but this *snkt!* is something I need to do singly. I believe he would have wanted *klkt!* a Saurish witness. And I am the closest thing to clanfolk his memory will have."

As I wait with Thea, I have a "clanfolk" question for her. "Thea, when you had us tell about our families . . . You've never mentioned your father."

She nods, while watching Clyne move slowly and carefully through Ungarth's things. "And perhaps now I never will."

"Why?"

"I don't know who he is. Mother said I couldn't know until I was older."

"Why was that?"

From nodding, she changes to shaking her head. "That's one of the secrets they killed when they took her. The answer is somewhere back in Alexandria. Waiting for me, perhaps. But I doubt I shall ever return. The fire took the city I knew." Before I can ask anything else, she continues. "And you, Eli, how come you wouldn't tell the bully who your mother is?"

"Because I think her real name is a war secret now. I didn't want him to know it."

"It's not just the bully who shares a fate with us."

"What do you mean?"

"It's Arthur and Ungarth, too. Time and history have broken all our families. All of us, except perhaps *him.*"

She points across the cave to Merlin. I don't know how he could have heard us, but he's nodding with a smiley expression like he's been part of the conversation all along. Thea suddenly walks over to Clyne and starts gathering things with him. He looks at her. Not mad, just curious about what she's up to.

"It's all right," she says to him. "Ungarth won't mind. I am the last of my kind, too."

Chapter Twenty-four

Eli: Time Boom

Somewhere in Old England & Dates Unknown

"What's the word again?"

"Sentient."

"But doesn't that mean it can think?"

"I've only been using it a short while, but yes, the vessel seems to be . . . if not quite making its own decisions, then augmenting mine."

"Doing stuff you didn't tell it to do?"

"Yes."

"Well, do you *trust* the ship?"

"I certainly trust K'lion's people. They built it."

"But do you trust the ship?"

Thea doesn't get to answer that question. We've loaded up all the items from Ungarth's cave into the Saurian time-craft, and Clyne has just loaded Rolf. We're saying our goodbyes to Merlin and Arthur.

"I still have something of yours," Merlin pulls my Seals cap out of his sleeve. I'm glad to see it's managed to become perfectly dry in the wizard's robes. I feel a bit doofusy for losing track of it, but then, I did have a gun pressed to my head.

I start to reach for the hat but realize that most of the Thickskin has come off. And I'd rather ride in the ship with Thea and Clyne.

"Thea, could you hang on to it, please?" I ask. "I don't have any covering for it right now."

She shrugs, then puts it on her own head. "My friend," she explains to Merlin, "has a symbiosis with this strange floppy helmet."

"It's a cap," I remind her.

"The cap serves as a key," she continues, "to unmoor him in time."

"That's always an option," I tell her. "If the ship spooks you, you and Clyne could hang on to my legs."

"I will trust the ship for a bit longer. Besides, we have the prisoner."

"Too bad, Thea. I was hoping we could moor you here for a while." It's Merlin again. He's nodding the same way he did in the cave, with that keeping-secrets-around-me-is-useless expression. "I would say, lass, you could learn a lot. But I suspect you could offer just as much."

Thea still isn't sure where she should go. Her real home, she says again, is gone.

"But your father could still be in Alexandria," I remind her.

"He could be. He could be anywhere else on Earth. He could be dead. And I'm not ready for the heartbreak of a fruitless search, Eli. Not now."

She doesn't want to come back with me, because every time she visits 2019, she gets shot at. And she doesn't want to spend her life explaining herself to Mr. Howe and his DARPA goons. I ask about Clyne's planet.

"I will return to Saurius Prime someday, because that's where the remnants of the Alexandrian library are. But though K'lion's people are generous, that's not quite home, either."

Arthur comes out of the ship after an impromptu tour from Clyne. "Amazing, Merlin. You should see it. I should have you conjure one for me—imagine the crusading we could do!"

"First, sire, you've a home to rebuild."

"Aye. And a sword to get reacquainted with." He raises Excalibur once more, which he's been doing a lot since we left the cave.

"Are you going to find your knights again?" I ask.

"Or let other knights find me. I do not know. 'Tis a different world from when we sat at the Round Table. I will rebuild the castle and see what happens next. But for now, I shall politely refuse to fade away."

And then I think: *But isn't that what happened? Didn't King Arthur just fade away? Did we change things by making him want to stick around? And if we just changed things, is it for the better?*

My dad mentioned a theory once that for every fork in the road, for every situation with more than one possible outcome—which is most of them—there's a new and parallel world created. A different one for each possibility. And each possibility after that. Which makes for an infinite number of forks in the road, and worlds to hold them.

First there's Mom, talking about how World War II was working itself out differently from the way it went the last time—and now this: King Arthur acting like he practically expects the cartoon Laddy to come riding up at any moment so that his royal adventures can continue.

I didn't want to keep making so many different worlds that I couldn't find my way back to my real home. Or that Mom and Dad would always have to stay apart.

"All is ready now for our swirly-bump voyage!" Clyne declares, emerging from the craft. He was referring to our plan to drop Rolf off somewhere in 1941, maybe with the U.S. or British Army. Then I would go back to Dad, in 2019. He must be pretty worried about me. Depending on when we touch back, I've been gone either a short time or a long time. I never know till I get home.

Thea finally decides to return to Saurius Prime with Clyne, at least for a while. "But perhaps when your castle is fixed, it could use a library," she says to Arthur and Merlin.

"Perhaps it could, m'lady. Perhaps it could." The king bows to us, and Merlin nods.

"My binding spell should be good on your captive for some time yet," the wizard adds. "But I am not entirely sure how sudden *chronological* changes affect it. Your ship's arrival shook him loose before. Be careful of sudden disruptions. I'll look forward to hearing about your journey next time." And then he bows, too.

Next time?

Stepping into the ship, I see how different it is from the "school model" Clyne had before. The body of the craft itself seems almost . . . liquid—walls and floors have shaped themselves into seats for all three of us.

Rolf is on a low bunk in the back. Part of the wall had oozed out to make restraints around him.

I take a seat and settle in. It makes itself snug around me. Thea is the pilot: She moves her hand over what must be a control panel—though really there are hardly any buttons or switches—and an area around it starts to glow.

"We need something to guide it back to that time of war," Thea says. "To give the ship a scent, so to speak."

"Well," I say as I look around, "what about

Rolf's uniform? It's the one he stole at Fort Point."

"Bring a piece up here. This seems to be where the vessel's . . . brains are. Though perhaps it's all becoming a single intelligence."

I try to tear a corner off Rolf's jacket, but it's too thick. "We need something sharp."

Rolf has been unusually quiet—considering how much he likes to brag. Merlin's spell didn't freeze his mouth, exactly, just reduced his voice to a whisper. But I'm close enough for him to try it out.

"We have weapons more terrible than this," he rasps. "This war is just beginning."

"This ship isn't a weapon."

Then he laughs. A croaky whisper-laugh, which gives me the creeps. "You always want everything to be so *nice,* Roy Rogers! Existence isn't *nice.* It is *fierce.* But you know that. You're not the good little cowboy you pretend to be. I see it in you. The dragon. You have it, too."

"I do *not*!"

"Don't listen to him," Thea tells me.

"Leave his word-salad alone," Clyne adds.

"You hear me, don't you, Roy Rogers? You know the truth. You would do what I do to survive. To prevail."

I can feel the anger inside me again. But I'm not like him. People who *are* like him always want to believe everyone else is the same way.

"Just shut up," I spit.

Then I see the knife.

It's jutting out from the ship wall, like the bunk, or the seats. The Saurian craft has manufactured it and appears to be . . . *handing* it to me.

But why? Why did it make a knife?

I snap it loose and use it to cut off a piece of Rolf's uniform. Is that why I have it? For a simple task? Or was the ship sensing something else?

In me?

No.

That's not who I am. No matter what Rolf

says. No matter what corny secret name Mr. Howe gives me. I'm just a twelve-year-old who wants to be home playing Barnstormers.

Right?

I hand the piece of cloth to Thea, who puts it on the control panel, which . . . absorbs it. She closes her eyes. "Find it," she whispers.

And I can tell by the feeling in my stomach that we've just burst into the Fifth Dimension.

Different parts of the ship swirl into translucent portholes outside, and I see the wildly vibrant colors streaking by in long lines—except for the ones that seem to explode in little pinwheels. Between the bursts of color, utter, utter blackness: the true opposite of light.

And then the sensations that come with it: a cross between giddiness and itchiness, memories seeming more alive than they ever have—almost as if they're dancing in front of you, like a portable Comnet screen.

Clyne, this time, just seems to be admiring the ship. "Gennt has once again stretched the ectoplasm of the possible!" he says, running his claws along the interior. Then he stops to consider. "But *tk!* I wonder if we'll be tested on any of this."

Thea still has her eyes closed, and she's still wearing my cap. It occurs to me that this ship, for her, is like a giant version of the Seals hat to me. The two halves of a time-traveling whole. Maybe not yet, but if the ship keeps thinking and changing like she says, could it grow to become part of her? What if she starts to need it for more than just travel?

My stomach's starting to quease out on me bigtime, so to take my mind off it, I try to make up a Barnstormer game in my head. Merlin is the new manager for my team, and I'll give him the power to alter one pitch each inning after it's been thrown—but one pitch only. And he can't wait till the inning's over and decide retroactively, either.

That lasts till somewhere in the top of the first inning—I can't concentrate. Then I remember the letter I have in my pocket, the one from Mom. Maybe that will help me focus. But it's not like this is an airplane ride and you can flip through a magazine. Even if I do get to read the letter, it will seem like a dream later.

I don't even know if the paper survived the last dunking in the lake. I fish around in my pockets and find the little mirror that woman was giving away at the Fairmont Hotel. The one from the old radio show. It seems like that was ages ago. Or ages from now? Hard to tell in the Fifth Dimension.

I finally come across the letter, a little scrunched up. It's covered in a plastic that feels like waxed paper, which is maybe all they had back then.

Dear lovely Sandman—

I'd completely forgotten about that nickname my mom had for Dad; no one's been around to use it for a long time. I know the letter's for him, and maybe I shouldn't read it. Maybe some things about your parents, you're not supposed to know.

I miss my beautiful family. I miss seeing our son grow. I miss how your eyes look in the morning.

WHAM!

The ship suddenly jolts.

I need to tell you things. Things I haven't been able to mention to anyone here. Things that scare me—

WHAM!

and will scare you, too.

I can't focus on the letter. I'm reading lines at random, and the whole thing is making me feel sad. Plus something's wrong with the ship. Thea's hands are knocked off the controls, and Clyne looks around to make sure we're okay. "Strange forces," he says. "Previously *ct!* unexperienced."

I check behind me, and Rolf is still fastened in. "What forces?"

"I don't know," Thea replies. "A wave . . . with an *emotional* charge. Did anyone else feel that strong pang of sorrow?"

"I felt a near-physical direction change,"

Clyne said. "Which is *snkk!* truly odd since there are no 'directions' in this sector of space-time."

Then I see what she added at Fort Point, and my stomach drops even more: *I don't know if I can ever come home . . .*

What? The line jumps out at me from the letter. I go back to re-read it before the next shock wave comes.

"Roy Rogers—"

I'm going to ignore Rolf. Though the sound of his creepy whisper has changed. . . .

ROLF!

I turn, and his eyes are bugging out. The bunk bed has completely oozed around him: He's being absorbed into the ship!

I must have shouted his name, because Thea and Clyne shoot over to me. As much as I despise this guy, I can't let the ship suck him up.

"The sword will still be ours someday. I'll come back for it."

That voice—his mouth isn't even moving.

It's . . . the ship. The *ship is speaking,* or somehow amplifying Rolf's thoughts as it sucks him into the walls. It's not that I'm crazy about saving Rolf—but I'm afraid of what could happen if the craft fuses with him.

I tug on his feet, but it's like he's slowly slipping underwater. I can see his face inside the walls of the ship.

I yank harder, but it's like pulling him out of a sea of glue. He's almost budging, but then . . .

The ship starts to suck *me* in! My arm is already inside the wall. . . .

"Thea!"

She's trying to pull me back, but it's not working. Besides, she and Clyne have to hop now, because the floor is getting sticky under their feet.

"Thea!"

"What, Eli?"

"Give . . . me . . . my . . . *cap.*"

"*What?*"

"The cap!"

I reach out with my free arm and just barely take it from her outstretched hand. I get it on my head right before my face is sucked into the ship's paneling, and *FOOM!*

It works.

My WOMPER-charged cap has popped me outside the ship—and I grab on, before I'm pulled away into one of the Fifth Dimension's swirling portals. I don't want to travel by myself. Like an astronaut on a space walk gone bad, I'm trying to stay connected to the ship until I can figure out what to do next.

Then a hand pops out of the ship's side.

It could only be Rolf's. I take it and keep pulling it through. With my other hand, I grab on to the rung of a ladder built into the ship's exterior. I eventually get a whole arm and part of a shoulder free.

I let go of the ship and float back into the void a little bit, while I keep hold of the arm, pulling. Eventually, I get his whole body out. "Hold on to me!" I yell. "We've got to try to get the others."

You have to shout, and even then, it still sounds like you're miles away.

I try to float us back toward the Saurian ship, which is now wildly morphing. The colors on the hull are changing rapidly, mirroring the colors outside. It makes a low, throaty singing sound, like a drawn-out moan.

I don't know what to expect from Rolf. There's no question he looks terrible. His hair is whiter and his face more pockmarked than the last time he came through the Fifth Dimension. And the journey isn't over yet. But even if I'm not holding my breath for a thank-you, I don't expect him to start scratching and clawing my face.

"No!" I shout at him. "Hold on to me!"

But Rolf keeps grabbing, kicking, and trying to throw punches. We're tumbling together, toward one of the color bursts looming behind him. It's too bright for me to look at directly . . . too intense.

But that gives me an idea. I reach into my pocket for the little mirror—while trying to hold him back. Rolf hangs on like a wolverine, and I can't take the chance that he might knock the cap off my head. I find the mirror and pull it from my pocket.

I glimpse the slogan inscribed on it—*You are reflected in your friends, family, and times*—then turn it toward Rolf's face, to reflect the light behind him. Except that it's not "light" as we know it.

The reflection doesn't bounce back into his eyes and distract him like I expected; instead it pours out of the mirror. The glass has now become another source of the color. And the colors begin enveloping his face.

It's enough to startle him into letting go. And in letting go, he's pulled into the swirling portal behind him. The last part of him I glimpse is his mouth forming a giant *NO!*

Without any kind of WOMPER-charge to guide him through the Fifth Dimension, I don't know what's going to happen to him. The antlers helped guide him back to Arthur's England last time. This time, for all I know, he could be stuck inside the Fifth Dimension forever.

The same way Thea and Clyne are stuck in the ship. I have to get back to help them. I turn my body as it's pulled through the dimensional currents and eddies—it almost feels like I'm swimming—and glimpse the ship below me. But it's hard to catch it, because another instant later, it's overhead. Then distant. Then close.

Things could go on this way until I pop out of this dimension, but the chase is interrupted with another loud *WHAM!* and this time the wave hits me directly.

The colors spin around me now, and I almost pass out, as another line from Mom's letter flickers in my mind—

We still have to find our way across time, to stay connected to what we love—and I'm clutching the little mirror, *One Man's Family,* and I realize that my family has grown. It's not just me and Mom and Dad anymore but Clyne and Thea, too, because we share the secret of this dimension together, of passing through epochs and eons, and centuries, and however far apart we are, the three of us are journeying *together* now somehow, no turning back, no matter what. . . .

I reach out and touch something smooth and sticky, like a wall of Jell-O. The side of the ship?

It's no longer a wall but someone's hand. Thea? Clyne? And the light falling on my face now comes with warmth. Heat. Light from a star. A sun.

I've come through the Fifth Dimension.

And as soon as I open my eyes, I will find out where.

ACKNOWLEDGMENTS

Books don't write themselves, much as authors might wish it sometimes, or as much as software makers might claim otherwise. Writers have to write them, but they have lots of help — friends and family to hold them near, or leave them alone when need be, and lots of colleagues who take the project into their own hearts.

During the seasons in which I revisited this story to make the edition you now hold, I am especially grateful to my sons, Elijah and Asher, for their constant inspiration; my friends Dick Bralver, Ellen Nadel, and Conrad Hurtt for shelter in the storm; Rick Klaw for a whole heap of scribe-specific moral support; and to Monica Perez, who so ably and deftly took the editor's reins on this project with enthusiasm, an eagle eye, patience, and humor. And speaking of holding this book in your hands, thanks, too, to designer Jeff Fresenius and artist Michael Koelsch for giving the Danger Boy series such a spiffy look.

Mark London Williams lives in Los Angeles, where he writes articles, comics, plays, and books. He says, "Every Danger Boy book has been fun to write. When my son Elijah was younger, he started to talk about dinosaurs and swords all at once, so the 'idea seeds' for this book were planted in my head. I hope the fun here is balanced with the seriousness of World War II and what it meant, and that readers will be as ready for the next Danger Boy adventure as I am!"

Eli's adventures continue in

Episode 3

Danger Boy

When a time-battered Eli Sands lands in the year 1804 at the launch of the famous Lewis and Clark expedition, he has no idea he's about to take part in the frontier adventure of a lifetime!

I believe I just talked with Thomas Jefferson. And I think Thea has been in to see me, too. But I was feverish when both things were happening, so I can't be sure.

And feverish or not, I don't know which is more surprising.

"What is happening in America that two young people show up out of nowhere, claiming to be lost, on such an otherwise pleasant afternoon?" I'm pretty sure I heard Jefferson

say that. He kind of likes to talk with extra words in his sentences.

"I won't let anything happen to you." That was Thea. She was dabbing cold rags on my head.

But even if it wasn't a dream, she's gone now, and there are guards outside the tent to keep me from leaving. I don't think I'm under arrest. I think they just don't know what to do with me yet.

And if I tell them the truth — that I'm from the future, that I've been tangled up in time after an accident in my parents' lab — well, they sure won't believe that my fever has passed. In fact, I might just find out where they lock up people they think are crazy or dangerous.

I don't even know how we got here. Where they don't study American history in books because they are *American history.*

Where they don't have baseball.

Where they don't even have Barnstormers! They don't have any Comnet games at all!

No wonder they had so much time to be historical and do famous stuff.